# ROYAL HOLIDAY

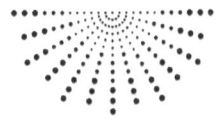

## CONSTANCE PHILLIPS

Edited by
GILLY WRIGHT
Cover artist
PAPER AND SAGE

CONSTANCE PHILLIPS PRESS

*Dream a dream, take a leap*

*This book is dedicated to those who care for humanity and dream of a better future for all.*

# CHAPTER ONE

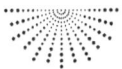

*T*he snow flittered down in front of the large plate glass window, easily distracting me from the task of stacking tins of my flavored coffee on the shelves.

January fourteenth.

Two weeks into the new year. Seven days after Epiphany.

The capital of Montgomery had turned into a virtual picture postcard.

Peaceful and Pretty.

The shop was quiet today, and there was a piece of me that welcomed the break. A week ago—during the peak of festival—we'd been bursting with customers from the moment the doors opened until I swept out the last stragglers well past our usual closing time.

Even though we'd had record-breaking sales during the last six weeks, the lack of customers today caused me worry. I had just clawed myself out of the sinking hole of debt. Maybe with the holiday season shopping behind us, my sales would decline. If so, how would I pay the bills?

I'd only opened *Viviana's Bistro*—named for my mother— nine months ago. It was an attempt to blend my memories of her and my passion for baking. If my memorial to the woman who'd shaped my life while working as a chef for the royal family failed, I wasn't sure I would recover from the disappointment.

Not to mention I'd be letting down my two employees, who needed their jobs as much as I needed to keep my mother's memory and recipes alive.

I tried to remind myself most people took some time to rest and recoup after the winter festival and Epiphany. Those who weren't taking time for themselves had probably returned to work. Things would pick back up in a few days.

They had to.

"Georgianne."

Hearing my name called turned my attention away from the floating flurries.

"What can I do for you, Mrs. Alscher?"

One of my best customers and the type of woman who considered herself everyone's grandmother. Her silver hair was streaked with traces of the black hair of her youth, but it was still impeccably styled.

"Could I trouble you for a refill?"

"Of course."

Every morning, Mrs. Alscher came into the shop precisely at nine. She ordered one of my freshly baked apple tarts—as if she knew they came from the oven at precisely eight fifty-five daily. She'd also order a cup of the special Montgomery roast coffee I blended myself, accented with a touch of sweet cream and a scant dash of sugar. She sat at the same table and read from a book or did needlepoint until eleven thirty.

She spoke to my customers and staff and seemed to know a little bit about what went on in everyone's life.

I only ever heard encouraging words and compliments

flow from her mouth. I'd never seen her angry or sad and never heard her speak a harsh word.

Like I said, she was everyone's grandmother. Though, she'd once told me, she and her husband had never been blessed with children.

I picked a sugar cookie from the case and took both it and the steaming coffee back to the table.

"Oh Georgie, you spoil me with your sweets."

"It looks like I over-baked today. It's better they are eaten. You don't want them to go to waste, do you?"

She closed her book and tapped the table on the other side of the small booth, inviting me to sit. "As quiet as it is, you must have some time to visit."

I couldn't say no and slid into the seat. "Business will pick up, I'm sure of it."

"Of course it will. And soon. Attendees for the summit sponsored by the queen's charity will be bringing child services employees and orphans from several nations." An exaggerated sigh escaped her. "To be young like our new king and queen and feel you can conquer the world."

I forced a smile. Upon marrying, the former king had abdicated his throne to his young son Sinclair and his new, American bride. The young couple were more beloved then his parents, as if it that were possible. The young queen had founded a charity benefitting orphans.

My father not only worked for Montgomery's children services, he headed our local agency. My entire life, we'd opened our home to foster children. Isabel and Marcus— both whom Dad had come to know through his work—had spent time in our home over the years. Giving them jobs when I opened the shop was like hiring family.

The thought of having to fire them squeezed my chest.

"More tourism," I whispered.

3

"Why do you look so sad? Surely, it will bring more customers for you."

"The summit is being held at the ski lodge, which is self-contained. There is no reason for anyone to leave in search of sweets and coffee." I tapped the woman's hand and slid out of the booth. "I need to make sure the bread gets in the oven. The lunch crowd should be coming in soon." *Hopefully.*

"I'll be needing one of those loaves, fresh from the oven. I finished my last bit with dinner last night."

"Sure thing."

In the kitchen, I moved the pans of rising bread dough—a dozen and a half of them—from the counter to the oven. Then, I set the timer and asked Marcus to keep an eye on them.

I returned to the front of the store to wipe down the counters and make sure all the tables were sparkly clean for the next rush. I'd just rinsed out my cloth, when the bell above the door sounded. I dropped it into the tub of hot water and bleach and wiped my hand on my apron as I approached the cash register. Looking up I saw a tall, blond —a rarity in Montgomery—man guiding eight young children into the shop as he held the door. He spoke to the children with a soft sternness, giving them directions in a language I didn't understand but sounded Eastern European.

From the corner of his eye, the stranger noticed Mrs. Alscher and, after giving the children a final direction in the foreign language, went to the table.

The kids lined up along the counter, facing me, with their hands neatly at their sides.

Mrs. Alscher's eyes lit up the moment she saw him. She stood, throwing her arms around his neck. He hugged her close, and the two whispered in the other language for a couple of minutes before he stepped up to the register and flashed the most beautiful baby blue eyes in my direction. He spoke in perfect English, accented with a dialect that confirmed my Eastern European guess. "I've been told you have the best hot chocolate in the city."

Pride welled in my chest, and I couldn't stop the smile. It felt good to know the people of this town not only appreciated my food and drink but also saw fit to tell others about their experience. "My own secret recipe."

"We'll have eight small mugs then, each with a chocolate chip cookie. And one super large cappuccino for me, please."

I called the order back to my staff and then turned my attention back to the chiseled man in front of me. Every time my eyes caught his sparkling blue ones, I felt as though my heart stopped beating. Wasn't it a sin to be so devilishly good looking? Certainly, it was wicked to lust after him. Yet, I couldn't seem to stop.

"This will take a few minutes. If you would like to have a seat, I can bring it out to you when it's all ready."

He gave me a curt not and spoke several short, incomprehensible words to the children, who walked in their straight line to the large table in the middle of the restaurant. They each took a seat and folded their hands on their laps.

I directed Isabel to begin making the children's drinks while I got out a stack of small saucers and placed a cookie on each one, arranging the dishes on my two larger trays.

"I wonder if they are here for the queen's summit," Isabella whispered under her breath as she put two mugs on a tray and then turned back to fill some more.

"I would say so." I answered. I didn't need to know a thing about the queen's charity to see what was happening in my bistro. I had heard the stern directions from a demanding social worker given to a scared child more times than I cared to remember. My father's staff had changed over the years. Some were warm and kind, others were like the man in front of me.

He might be sizzling hot, with the kindest eyes I'd ever seen, but the stern voice told me he ruled with an iron fist. I wondered how harsh he would become if one of child stepped out of line.

I felt so bad for the children. How awful to live in a constant fear.

As I carried the tray over to the table, I studied the solemn faces of the children. Kids shouldn't look that way, especially so soon after Christmas and Epiphany.

"I hope you like chocolate chips," I tried to make conversation as I set plates in front of each child.

Tall, blond, and striking leaned back against another table, his arms folded across his chest.

I paused in front of a boy who appeared to be about six years old. His shaggy brown hair was clean, yet overgrown, nearly covering his eyes. He looked up and under his bangs, and I could see sadness resonating in his deep brown pools.

After I had placed his food and drink on the table, the child spoke softly—yet clearly—in the same language the social worker spoke.

"What's your name?" I asked.

He tilted his head and didn't seem to understand what I'd said.

Had the queen thought of that when she'd decided to bring the orphans of the world together for a big playdate?

"Steven." That was the blond Adonis.

"You are Steven?"

He shook his head and motioned to the child. "Steven doesn't speak English…or Italian. We are working with him —all of them—on expanding their language skills." After a pause, he continued. "My name is Layton."

I nodded to him and continued passing out the cookies and hot chocolate. Despite knowing the kids couldn't understand me, I spoke warmly to each one. Believing they were scared, I wanted them to feel like this was a safe place.

The social worker served as translator, both to the children and to me. With each one I spoke to, the group warmed up. Frowns became smiles, and they began to speak softly to each other.

The last cup on this tray went to the last child sitting on this side of the table. She appeared to be about six years old, just like Steven. She had straight blond hair that was bluntly cut so it fell just below her cheekbone. He blue eyes sparkled. Unlike the others, she seemed almost happy.

"Thank you, miss," the girl said.

Layton stepped forward. "Hannah is the exception to the rule. She speaks English very well."

I squatted down so I was eye level with the child. "You are very welcome, Hannah. Go ahead and taste the cocoa and let me know what you think."

She looked up to Layton with her large pleading eyes, and his rough edges melted before my eyes.

He squatted down on the opposite side of her and nodded, before turning his gaze on me.

Had I been too quick to judgment? Would this sweet little girl look at Layton with such adoration if he were as cold as I first thought?

Hannah lifted the cup to her lips and took a long sip, her smile growing wider.

"It's very good."

"I'm so glad you like it."

Isabel showed up with a second tray filled with enough drinks and cookies to feed the rest of the children, and one large cappuccino for Layton. After serving the little ones, I tucked the now empty tray under my arm and handed him his cup. He nodded to me but gave his full attention to the kids. He spoke to them in their native language, less stern, but in no way gentle.

In unison, the kids all said *Thank you* to me.

Adonis smiled and clapped his hands. "*Ya! Ya! Essen.* Eat."

I started to retreat to the kitchen when I felt as though I was being followed. Sure enough, the social worked slid up onto one of the stools at the counter.

"Thank you."

"It's not a problem. Serving food and drink is what we do here."

He nodded and cocked his head. "*Ya.* I expected that, I didn't not necessarily expect warmth and kindness to the children. A man with eight young ones is not always welcome in bistros. Or restaurants of any kind, for that matter."

I knew he spoke the truth. "Despite what some people think, kids should be kids, not programmed robots."

"You think I'm too harsh with my children?"

"They're only that age once, it'd be a shame if they can't experience joy or merriment—especially this time of the year."

He took a long sip from his mug but never took his eyes off me. He seemed to be trying to look through my flesh. It made me feel weak, exposed, and totally vulnerable to him.

"I don't disagree with you. However, it is my job to make sure these children have all the best advantages. When it comes to finding homes, a well-mannered child has a better chance than one who isn't."

Another point I couldn't deny. Still, it pained my heart. All children deserved a home.

A mother.

A father.

All should know where their next meal would come from and have a safe and warm place to sleep at night.

My eyes drifted back to the children. They were clean and neat, but their clothes were well worn. I remembered the many children of that age who came in and out of our home. Many wanted nothing more than a new toy or a set of clothes that was all theirs first, just one item that had never belonged to another person

I was sure these kids felt the same way. "Sometimes even the best-behaved little angels still end up lost."

"That sounds like you're speaking from experience."

I nodded slightly. "Nothing special though. We all have lived through incidents that shaped us."

Layton the social worker's all-about-business look had softened while I was talking to the children. Now, his eyes morphed again, filling with sadness. "As lovely as our beautiful hostess is, I won't keep them here long. I do appreciate the distraction. When I found out our rooms at the lodge were not ready, I wasn't sure how I was going to entertain them."

"One would think the queen would have things better organized."

Layton visibly bristled. "You take issue with Queen Margaret."

"I have nothing but respect and high regard for the entire royal family, including our new queen. I just question the effectiveness of a multicultural playdate in a ski lodge. Couldn't the money that is being spent be better used to provide clothes, food, housing, toys? Or it could help to educate the public as to the need for more foster and adoptive families? Now, to hear this effort isn't even well organized..."

"I said no such thing. In fact, it is quite the contrary. They were able to check us into the summit, get me my packets, and—when our room wasn't ready because we are four hours early—directed me to this charming little bistro with a spitfire for a waitress."

"Owner." I clarified. "I'm Georgianne Bosco."

He extended his hand across the counter. "Nice to meet you."

I hesitantly took it, somehow knowing his flesh would be silk soft and warm. Despite my first impressions, the longer we talked I learned Layton cared about people. Behind the armor he wore, a gentle kindness oozed from his every pore.

"It's nice to meet you too." Thank heavens for polite auto responses. If I'd had to think up an answer on my own, I'm sure I would have stood there—mouth agape—staring at his strong, chiseled jaw.

"You know, this summit is a lot more than a multicultural playdate, as you called it. Her royal highness is providing us with educational materials and access to funding. By bringing us all together, and having each nation bring some of its orphaned children, it is raising awareness and attention. The plight of these children is a difficult subject for most folks. The press is hesitant to report on their day-to-day struggles. It often gets swept under the figurative rug. I would say your average citizen doesn't have a clue how many children are left homeless and without care. Everyone has room in their hearts for an infant..."

I'd lowered my stare to the counter. He was passionate about a cause near and dear to my heart. Having shared our home over the years with the children Layton spoke about, I'd never taken for granted my loving family. Conversations with my father about his work, went much the same way this one with Layton had. It was a universal problem. One that needed a spotlight shined on it.

Layton must have sensed my sadness. He paused and took a drink of his cappuccino. "I'm sorry. I didn't mean to preach."

I lifted my chin and pasted on another smile. "The world needs more Laytons."

"Why thank you." He bowed slightly.

I heard a bustling sound and looked to see Mrs. Alscher gathering her things. She then approached the counter. She reminded me the lunch crowd would be arriving soon.

*Hopefully.*

"My bread!" I twisted out on my heels and started to call out to Isabel, only to find her standing in front of me with Mrs. Alscher's order already packaged.

"Everything is fine, Georgie. Marcus took over the lunch prep. We'll be ready for the rush."

"Let's just hope we have one today," I whispered before gripping Isabel's hand. "Thank you so much. I don't know what I'd do without you two. Mrs. Alscher, I'll meet you at the register."

She didn't detour her path and continued straight for me. "There's no need for that, my dear. I order the same thing every day and get the bread once a week. I'm also well aware of what a sugar cookie costs." She slid a folded bill across the counter "You keep the change, sweetie."

I handed her the bag in my hand. "I will do no such thing. The dessert was my treat."

"You give such fine service, you deserve the tip." She slid a bit closer to Layton. "Doesn't she, Prince?"

*What?* "Mrs. Alscher, this is Layton, he's—"

"A prince. Son to Edgar and Kirsha, ruling Monarch of Ronaria. He's also my cousin. How is your dear mother, by the way?"

Layton chuckled and carefully hugged the woman again. "Alma. I'm so sorry. I'd intended to make my way back to talk to you. Must you leave now?"

"Do I look like a woman who has nothing to do and nowhere to go." Mrs. Alscher always seemed so upbeat and positive that the genuine look of sadness in her eyes threw me off guard.

"But how often do you and I get the chance to visit. Please say you will come out to the lodge this afternoon so we can catch up."

"Of all your brothers, you've always been the most kind and charitable. You've grown into a fine young man."

He laughed again. "I think my mother deserves the credit for that. She is the one who raised me."

Alma shook her head and laid her hand on his shoulder. "And modest too. How is it some young lady hasn't snatched you up?"

He winked at her. "They try, but I'm rather slippery."

She laughed as if he'd told the funniest joke she'd ever heard. "You give my best to your mother. And Queen Margaret, when you see her as well. I would have loved to be involved in this summit."

"Let me see what I can arrange." He picked up a napkin off the counter and pulled a pen from the inside pocket of his jacket. "Give me a couple of hours to get the kids settled and then come out. Maybe we can have dinner. If I can't get you into the summit, I at least want you to come out to the opening session in the morning as my special guest."

She waved her hand in front of her face, shaking her head. "These days I'm best served holding down my booth here at Georgianne's lovely bistro."

After handing Alma the napkin he'd written on, he lifted his mug from the counter taking a sip. "She does make a wicked good cup of cappuccino." He looked over his shoulder to the table, "And the children have devoured their hot chocolate and cookies."

"You won't hear a complaint from anyone." She turned to face me. "Thank you again for a lovely breakfast and the company, Georgianne. Unless I take Layton up on his offer, I will see you tomorrow."

"I will be here."

Once Mrs. Alscher had left, my gaze landed back on Layton. So, Adonis just happened to be a prince, and I'd been so belligerent and judgmental. "I owe you an apology," I bowed slightly. They way my parents had taught me was proper when in the company of royalty.

He waved his hand in front of him. "Please, no formalities. I'm the same person you thought I was a few minutes ago."

"A social worker?"

He laughed again. Soft. Musical. It made a slew of butterflies in my stomach beat their wings and take flight.

"I thought I was up to speed on this summit. The news made it sound like the children would be accompanied with agency people."

"I am the head of our nation's children services division, so I guess your assumption wasn't too far off base."

"You have enough time for such work?"

"It is my only work. It is my debt of gratitude to the nation my family serves."

"The children mean a lot to you?"

"They mean the world. From the way you treated my kids, I can tell you have a fondness for children as well."

"Very much so."

"I bet you were raised in a large family." He had a glint in his eye telling me he believed he was good at reading people.

"Not at all. I'm an only child."

"I'd love to know more about you and your family."

"I'm sure you don't have time. You must have to get back to the summit soon."

He glanced down at his watch. "You are not wrong." He spun on his heels, and directed words spoken in his natural tongue to the children. His voice held the same sternness—authoritativeness—it had when he first showed up. The kids reacted immediately, neatly stacking their cup on the saucer. They then stood, pushed their chair back up to the table and slid on their coats, scarves, hats, and gloves before forming two by two lines in front of the door.

Layton then turned back and face me. "How much do I owe you?"

I had forgotten all about making out their bill. "Oh, let me see."

Isabel nervously approached. "I rang up the order for you, Georgianne, and then suspended it in the register"

"Thank you. You, my friend, are a saint." *Please, lord, give me a good lunch rush. Don't put me in a position to have to lay her off.*

I motioned to the Prince of Ronaria to follow me down the length of the counter, and he gladly did. With the tap of a few buttons on the cash register I had his bill called up.

He offered me a credit card that was like none I'd ever seen. Simple black, with a series of numbers. No name. No bank insignia. A small, generic crown in the lower corner. I tipped it back toward him ready to question whether my bank would accept it.

He interrupted before I could say a word. "I'm positive the card will process just fine."

I shrugged my shoulders, deciding it didn't hurt anything to try. True to Layton's words, *approved* lit up my display in record speed.

I ripped away the receipts the machine spit out and offered them to Layton with his card. "I need you to sign the top one."

He picked a pen up off the counter and scribbled his name illegibly. "Thank you, Georgianne, for the best cup of cappuccino I've had in as long as I can remember. I hope to see you again while I'm in your fine country."

If he'd shown those manners when he first walked into the bistro, I might have guessed him a prince. Instead, he'd acted so down to earth it hadn't even crossed my mind. I tried to rationalize that I didn't expect him because I knew the faces and names of our own royalty—and many of their extended relatives and the regularly visiting fellow nobles. Not because they graced my coffee shop, but because my mother's job in the castle bred familiarity.

Trying to shake off my thoughts, I looked down at the receipt. He'd written in a more than generous tip. He'd also drawn an arrow, encouraging me to flip over the receipt.

*Thank you for accepting my children with warm hospitality. I would love to talk to you some more. Please join me in the restaurant at the lodge at eight tonight for coffee and dessert. I'm sure it won't be as sweet as anything you would make, but I hesitate to be too far away from my children.*

# CHAPTER TWO

Two o'clock came quickly, and my father strolled in just minutes before I twisted the lock on the door. We'd had a decent lunch crowd—enough for me to avoid laying off my loyal staffers. It hadn't been overwhelming though, so I sent Marcus and Isabel home, telling them I could handle the clean-up on my own.

As I made my father his usual lunch—turkey sandwich with extra mustard—I thought back to Layton's invitation. I hadn't yet decided if I would take him up on it. What business did I have going on a date with a prince?

Quickly, I tried to set the teenaged me aside. Layton had never used the word date. He'd asked me to join him for coffee and desert so that we could *talk*.

"Will you join me today?" My father asked as I set the plate in front of him at the counter.

I looked over my shoulder and through the small window to the kitchen. I had work to do, but it wouldn't take me long.

"I would love to. Why don't we sit at a table? It will only take me a minute to grab some food."

Back in the kitchen, I scooped some egg salad onto a plate and then added a spoonful of diced fruit. I snatched my cup of water from under the counter and joined my father at the table in front of the window.

It didn't surprise me he picked the one bathed in sunlight. Spending his days in a cinder block office, he migrated toward fresh air and natural light much as he could.

"I have to say; I sort of expected you to be up at the summit today."

"It doesn't officially start until tomorrow morning. I will be the rest of the week." He sighed, took another bite of the sandwich and chewed it thoroughly before swallowing. Before he spoke, he wiped his mouth with a napkin. "Today is mostly an arrival day. There is a welcome dinner tonight I'm obligated to attend."

If my father felt duty-bound to be there, Layton must need to attend too. As had happened all day, my mind rolled back to tall, built, and blond. Remembering his dimpled chin and wide shoulders made my stomach quiver. "But it will be all over by eight?"

He nodded, but the look on his face clearly wondered how I'd known that. "One of the attendees brought some children in for a hot chocolate and cookies this morning. We got to talking, and he invited me out to the lodge for coffee this evening." Why did I hold back that my customer was Prince Layton? Maybe because I was still processing that bit of information myself

Father's eyebrow peaked, but he didn't rush to speak. He took a long sip of his milk and then took another bite of his sandwich. "Where is this *man* from?"

"Ronaria." It didn't even cross my mind to hide that last bit. My father and I had always been close, but since my mother's accident, we relied on each other too much to keep secrets.

I could see the wheels of his mind spinning. He eye's perked up again. "Prince Layton?"

It was bad enough that I'd spent all afternoon imagining myself with the handsome prince, I didn't need my father imagining it too. "You know him?"

"Of him," he corrected. "I've never had the pleasure of meeting him."

*Pleasure.* "You approve of his work?"

"Why wouldn't I? We're all working for the same common cause."

I was confused. My insolence about this summit had been fueled by listening to my father's rantings. "The way you talked about this summit made me believe you weren't so happy about it."

He frowned. "I don't like being called away from my desk for several days. And I shudder to think about the amount of money that's being spent. I have a long list of unfunded programs that would greatly benefit from a fraction of the queen's budget for the next few days. *However,* there is a lot of good that can come from a meeting of the minds. No doubt this will bring international attention to our common goal." He paused and took another sip of his milk. "You don't need me to keep prattling on. I'm sure Prince Layton will tell you anything else you need to know."

"I haven't even decided for sure if I'm going."

"Why would you refuse?"

"Why would I accept? Whatever would we talk about?"

My father set his drink down and looked me in the eye. "He must have something in mind, or he wouldn't have invited you."

"You're not worried about exactly what that something might be?"

At that moment, my father smirked. *An actual smirk!* "You are an adult."

"Father!" We were close, yes, but my relationships weren't something we usually discussed. Maybe that was because it had been a long while since I had one. Opening the bistro not only took financial resources but had also been physically and emotionally draining on me. I had no time for a personal life. I hadn't dated at all since the day I opened the doors here, and to say I was lonely was an understatement.

"From what you said, he's invited you to a public place for a cup of coffee and conversation. Very polite. Very appropriate first date."

"Who said anything about date?"

"You said *what would we talk about*, but if I know my daughter—as I believe I do—you talked his ear off while he was here."

"And those of the children..."

He nodded as if it all made sense now. "From what I hear in business circles, Layton is very dedicated to his job."

"Those children seemed like more than a job to him. I found it surprising that a prince oversaw their country's children's services program."

"He has older brothers. Five of them, in fact."

"He's a spare then."

"He's the spare's spare's spare."

"Father! That's rude."

"Maybe, but it's true." He chuckled again, amused by his own joke. "Ronaria is a very poor country. Their resources are even more limited than ours. All members of their royal family head up humanitarian departments. For most, it's a job. For Layton—I understand—it is his heart's passion."

It certainly seemed so to me.

In silence, my father quickly finished and then gathered his dishes and stood. "I'm going to put these in the kitchen and head back to work. I'll let you get to your clean-up and shut-down so you can prepare for your date."

"It's not a date," I protested, even though I couldn't stop wondering what I would wear.

———

$\mathcal{M}$y mind was still preoccupied with Layton—the things he'd said and the words my father and Mrs. Alscher had shared with me. Two people I cared very much about had given this man a stamp of approval.

*He'll only be in this country for a few days. I'm sure romance is the last thing on his mind.*

The logical side of me tried to squash my desires. I knew so much stood in the way of this being any more than a friendly evening between two people.

Distance for one.

After the summit, there would be a great many miles separating us. Technology had a way of making the world a smaller place. So maybe that one could be overcome. But what about the fact that he was royalty and my family had spent their lives serving our country's crown.

*That* had to make us incompatible. Didn't it?

*He only invited you to have a single cup of coffee and some dessert.*

*You're the only one thinking it's something more!*

After locking up the restaurant, I went straight home and took a long shower. I carefully did my hair and makeup, despite the fact the voice in my gut continued to protest.

Even if it wasn't a date, I wanted to look my best. I longed for him to look at me the way he had while I talked to the children.

A quick glance at the clock told me that time was drawing near, so I dressed in a gray wool sweater dress, black leggings, and gray knee-high boots.

I touched up my hair, added another coat of hairspray to

keep my unruly curls in some sort of style and retraced my path down the steps and out to my car in what seemed like record time.

It was Montgomery in January. Snow was always in the forecast and on the ground. Tonight was no exception.

The light snow continued to fall, making the roads a bit slick, but it wasn't too far to the Lodge, and the drive was uneventful.

Upon arrival, I hiked from my parking spot toward the entrances. I was held back from the door for a few minutes as a security detail cleared a path for King Sinclair and Queen Margaret to make their exit to a waiting sedan.

As the car whisked out of the parking lot, I entered the lodge to the restaurant where I was to meet Layton.

I was surprised by the number of the children who ran through the lobby, though I supposed I shouldn't have been. I had heard on the news reports—and Layton had confirmed—all the summit's attendees were bringing orphans from their countries.

It did my heart good to hear such merriment, and the children—some playing board games, others running around playing chase—all seemed to be enjoying their time away from their usual institutions.

No one was happier than me to see the children happily socializing despite their language barriers.

At the door to the ballroom, a frazzled hostess asked to see my conference credentials.

"I'm meeting someone," I explained and let my eyes scan the restaurant. Immediately, my gaze locked on to Layton. Having exchanged the jeans and sweater he wore earlier for a formal tuxedo, he stood near the bar—looking even more scrumptious than he had in my bistro. A line had formed of people wishing to speak to him, but it was the person at the front that grabbed my attention.

My father.

He'd said he'd always wanted to meet Prince Layton and obviously seized the opportunity tonight. I wondered if the fact his royal highness had asked me to coffee played a part in my father's introduction.

"Thank you, I've found him."

As I closed the distance between Prince Layton and me, I felt my head grow light. It seemed so surreal.

As if he could feel my stare, he pulled his attention from my father and met my gaze. A large smile lit up his face. He turned back and offered to shake my dad's hand.

I was close enough now to hear him speak. "I'm so happy we finally got a chance to meet, Mr. Bosco. I do hope we get a chance to talk some more tomorrow."

"It would be my pleasure."

Dad reached out wrapping an arm around my shoulder. "There's my girl."

I returned my father's embrace, even though it was out of place for him to show affection—or pride for that matter. Not that I ever believed he was ashamed or embarrassed by me, but he'd never gone out of his way to introduce me to a business associate.

I gave my attention to the prince. "Am I early? It seems like the event is still going on."

"You are right on time, and I'm so glad you decided to come. It will be like this for the next four days." He turned to my father. "If you would please excuse us."

Layton then turned to those who had formed a line behind my father. "My apologies. I do hope you will understand. I will be happy to speak with all of you later, but I don't want to keep Miss Bosco waiting."

He offered me his elbow and escorted me out of the restaurant.

Every eye in the place seemed to be burning into us. Was

it possible to feel embarrassed and be so deliriously happy at the same time? That odd mixture was exactly what was churning up my insides.

"I thought we were going to have coffee." I hadn't known what type of label to put on this evening, but I believed we were meeting for dessert. It hadn't occurred to me coffee and desert had been a euphemism for climb between the sheets.

Even as I tried to push the idea away, my cheeks flushed with the thought of being lip-locked with the rugged man on my arm.

His chuckle tickled my ear. "Of course. I'm sure you noticed, we would have not a moment to ourselves in the main dining room. I requested, and was granted use of, one of the conference rooms. The staff has set up coffee and dessert. I do hope you don't mind me ordering for you, but I can't bear to be in Montgomery and not have some tiramisu."

"Thank you. I've heard it's a specialty of the lodge."

"You've never had?" He led me down a hall that ran off the main lobby. About a quarter of the way down the corridor, he opened the door on the left.

The room still looked to be set up for a lecture or seminar. Rows of chairs in front of an eight-foot, rectangular table in the front of the room. A white screen stood behind the table. On top of a typical black table cloth was a white place setting with two mugs of steaming coffee and two plates of the rich dessert.

We crossed the room, and Layton held my chair.

After he sat across from me, I answered his question. "I don't really have a lot of time for skiing."

"I imagine running your business is very time-consuming. Still, you should take an occasional break to enjoy life."

"The bistro is very new and still taxing on all my resources." I hadn't meant to say the words out loud, but my stress about the declining sales had set up permanent residence in my mind. No matter what was said to me, I found some way to twist it into how it affected my coffee shop. When asked a direct question, how could I not honestly answer?"

His face contorted to a frown. It seemed he wasn't sure how to take what I had said. Thankfully, it was fleeting. "Well, you served me the best cappuccino I've ever had and the kids had nothing but good things to say about their treats as well."

My cheeks warmed, and I looked away, not wanting him to see my blush. "That's very kind of you."

"It's the truth."

"I do my best to provide good food and service." My response sounded lame, even to me. What I wanted to say was, *tell all your friends. Send them my way so I can make my mortgage payment and keep my employees.* But, I would never ask for help from anyone, let alone a prince. I realized most of the people in line wanting to speak to Layton had a request of him. He was probably used to it, but it must get old to constantly be asked for help.

"Running a coffee shop is a huge undertaking."

"Not as big as being a prince, I'm sure."

He waved his hand in front of his face. "With five older brothers, there isn't much responsibility that falls to this spare."

"My father's description of running a country's children services program doesn't exactly sound like a vacation at the beach."

"It does keep me busy, but I enjoy it."

"I feel the same way about my bistro."

"Sometimes, I fear, this face gets in the way of me doing the best job I could."

What was he trying to say? Did he really believe the fact that he was drop-dead gorgeous meant he couldn't handle the work? What did it say about him if he realized just how attractive he really was? I felt my eyebrows knit together making my confusion evident. Maybe the prince had an ego he hadn't shown me yet.

His hand came across the table landing on mine. The left corner of his mouth hiked up a bit, causing his cheek to dimple. "What I meant to say is my notoriety. If my parents weren't who they are, I wouldn't have had a line forming to speak to me. I wouldn't have had people passing me notes through dinner and whispering their requests for help in my ear. People assume because of my bloodline; I have a well-funded program that doesn't face the same issues theirs does."

I dipped my fork into the dessert and lifted the tiniest of bites to my mouth. While the rich creamy flavor accented with bold coffee caressed my taste buds, I thought about how we had polarizing problems. I'd give anything for a little bit of exposure for my little bistro, and he'd love to be another face in the crowd.

He dipped his chin, so he could meet my gaze. "Was it something I said? You seem so far away."

I swallowed. "Not at all. I was just thinking about our similar problems. I feel ineffective in my job too, but because no one notices me."

"You have poor sales?" He seemed shocked.

Now I felt bad for exposing my dark cloud to what was supposed to be a nice evening. "I seem to find a way to make ends meet." *Most days.*

"It's hard to make a good living on *making ends meet.*"

*Exactly.* Let alone paying my employees. "Sales were great during the holidays. It allowed me to catch up on all the bills I was behind on. Now, things are starting to slow down again. If it doesn't improve soon, I may have to layoff Isabel and Marcus. Father will be so disappointed if it comes to that."

Layton shook his head, "I don't believe that. He seemed very proud of you when we were spoke earlier."

"He's delighted I've been able to hire two of his charges who aged out of foster care. As far as my choice to open a bistro, I'm not so sure he's as pleased."

He tipped his head, and the admiration in his eyes deepened. "You hired young adults out of your country's children's services program?"

"It was his idea actually. He had a hundred and one reasons why I should try and get a job in another restaurant instead of opening my own, until I mentioned I would need at least two employees from day one. He suggested Isabel and Marcus. I already knew them well. They'd come to live with us off and on over the years. Dad told me they were struggling to set up housekeeping since aging out of the system."

"And you just hired them. That is an incredible and kind thing to do."

My cheeks warmed again. "They are like family to me. They're good people and hard workers. It would kill me to have to let them go."

"Could you run the bistro all by yourself? It seems like a lot for one person."

And that was the conundrum I hadn't really faced head on yet. "I would have to give it my best shot, but truthfully, it would be hard. I don't see how I can wait on customers, prepare the orders, and continue to have the same consistency in quality I've had until now."

"Seems like an insurmountable task to me."

I shrugged my shoulders and tried to smile. "It beats failing. I'd have to try."

We sat there in silence for a moment. He studied my

features. I couldn't pinpoint what was going on behind those crystal blue eyes, and he didn't quite seem ready to share.

I wanted to kick myself for spilling my guts. Here I was given the opportunity to spend some time with a handsome man and I chose to dump my problems at his royal doorstep.

I took a large gulp from my coffee, that had now grown cold. "I'm so sorry. I shouldn't have bothered you with my troubles. You were kind enough to invite me here—"

"To get to know you."

*Really?* "And here I thought it was because you wanted my opinion on the coffee and dessert."

"Well, that too." He shot me a wink. "You didn't know who I was until Alma told you. Did you?"

Embarrassed, I shook my head. "I really do feel like I keep up on the world stage."

"Please don't apologize. It is just one of the many things about you I find intriguing."

"That I didn't know who you were at first?"

"Or didn't hold me to a higher standard because of it. You even seemed irritated with me at first. After being pandered to for so many years, it's quite refreshing."

I couldn't help but laugh. "You want someone to give you attitude?"

"Well, maybe not that far—I'm not a masochist—but you didn't hold back your feelings. With me, and the children too. As you might imagine, I run into people every day who are not authentic. They only tell me the things they think will please me."

"I can see how that would get old pretty fast."

"Yes, it does."

"So you wanted to get to know the person who didn't know you."

"The beautiful lady who didn't have a preconceived notion of who I was or what I was about. The woman who

27

was kind to my children and could fix an amazing cup of coffee."

"You keep going on about coffee, I'm beginning to think you have an addiction."

He raised his hands in front of his chest and laughed. "Guilty as charged." After a pause, he stood. "Come, let us go outside for a walk."

I stood and retrieved my jacket from the back of the chair. "It's getting late."

He gave me a sheepish look, like he believed I was just making some excuse. Who knows. Maybe I was. I was enjoying just spending time with Layton. If we continued to talk—to connect—I would only grow fonder of him. Then what happened at the end of the summit when he had to leave? He went back to his nation and left me here with my café.

He slipped behind me and helped me with my coat. "If you must go, what can I say."

He hovered over me, so close I could smell his earthy cologne and feel the heat of him assaulting my senses. As crazy as this was, I didn't want to leave him. Couldn't just yet. "I have a little time yet. Let's walk."

# CHAPTER THREE

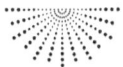

*A*fter sliding another tray of banana muffins into the oven, I picked up my now empty coffee cup and returned to the large percolator, refilling it with the dark roast.

Even though I knew I had to come in early, leaving Layton had been hard. We went for a long walk along the trail toward the ski lifts. The night was cold and clear, but I didn't notice the chill in the air, especially when he wrapped his arm through mine and encased my hand with his.

I asked him more about his country, remembering what my father said about it being a poor nation. Layton confirmed it, telling me about his struggle to get any funding to improve the children's lives. The orphanage had the necessities, so the kids' needs were met, but Layton longed to give them enriching experiences. He hoped our queen's new program would help him enact some of his ideas.

It wasn't until we crossed back through the lodge, and Layton had walked me to my car, that I realized it was nearly midnight.

I only managed to get three hours sleep before I had to

head into work. My father had been in bed long before I got home and still slept when I left again. I hadn't had the chance to ask him about what he and Layton were discussing. Since he would be at the summit today, I wasn't sure I would get a chance to talk to him until much later.

Sleepy? Yes. But, it was more of a dreamlike state. Layton hadn't touched me beyond an occasional grip to my hand, but the longer we spoke, the closer I felt we were growing, sharing such passion for the work we did, while facing many of the same obstacles.

I shook off my lingering daydreams and, with coffee in hand, went into the kitchen to check on the daily soups, just as the back door opened and Isabel and Marcus walked in.

After a few minutes of light chatter, they both clocked in and when straight to work.

Knowing they had the kitchen under control, I used a pair of tongs to pick up one of the fresh cinnamon rolls from the tray and let them know I was going to have a seat in the dining room and enjoy my breakfast.

I didn't often do this. Usually I ate something substantial before coming in, hoping not to be tempted by my pastries and sweets, but today something dripping in sugar was what I required—maybe my taste buds were jealous of my sappy heart.

The warm sugar and cinnamon mixed with the boldness of the dark roast coffee and made feel cozy.

I was nearly done with the roll when I heard a tap on the window and saw Mrs. Alscher at the door. She had a colorful scarf wrapped around her head and wore a long, black wool coat over a dress and a pair of tights.

I wondered why she was dressed so smartly and out so early.

I didn't open for another half hour, but I couldn't refuse my most loyal customer.

I slid out of the booth and crossed the dining room, twisting open the lock. "Come in out of the cold."

"Thank you so much for opening up, sweetheart. My dear cousin pulled some strings and made it possible for me to attend the summit. I would like to take a selection of your pastries and danishes. Do you have anything ready?"

"I do." I walked behind the counter. "I have cinnamon rolls, cannoli, lemon tarts, and apple blossoms ready right now. I'll have apple and banana muffins in another fifteen minutes."

"I don't have time to wait. I'll take a half dozen of each item you have ready now."

"*Each?*"

She gave me a large toothy smile that lit up her whole face. "Why are you so surprised?"

"You realize that is two dozen pastries."

She tipped her head, and her mouth squeezed to a pucker. "Maybe you're right. I should get a total of three dozen. Add three of each kind. Oh, and I'll have a large coffee with cream and sugar to go."

I could hardly believe my ears. Mrs. Alscher's order was going to clear me out of current stock. I had muffins in the oven, but I would at least need some tarts and cannoli. I rang up the order and my godsend pseudo-grandmother happily paid.

I turned back to the display case to begin filling boxes, but I first leaned through the window separating the dining room from the kitchen and called out to Isabel to start making crust for tarts and cannoli shells.

After packaging the order, I prepared her a coffee to her tastes, the very same way I'd been making it since the first day she came in. Since the first day I opened my doors.

On a whim, I filled a second to-go cup with coffee as well, adding enough cream, sugar, and caramel syrup to make it as sweet as the cappuccino Layton had ordered the day before.

I picked up the black sharpie by the register and wrote his name on the side. "Could you please deliver this to Layton for me?"

Mrs. Alscher gave me a knowing look, apparently seeing through what I thought was an innocent act of kindness. Even if some part of me knew I was hoping to keep the lines of communication open with the prince.

"You two seemed to be getting along quite well yesterday."

"He is very kind." *And smart. And generous. And did I mention handsome?*

She dipped her chin. "He is that. A true humanitarian." She slid her arm through the corded handle of the brown paper bag holding her pastries and picked up a cup in each hand. "I will be more than happy to deliver this for you."

"Thank you."

"Don't give it another thought. I will see you tomorrow morning." With that she gave me her little goodbye wave I'd come to love and ushered herself out of the store.

It was as if having the summit had given her a purpose. I'd never sensed something was missing her life until I saw her walk taller with her shoulders erect and squared. Even her ever-present smile seemed to shine brighter.

Still, she hadn't forgotten about me or the shop. I didn't doubt she wanted to take something to the summit to thank Layton for his kindness; it was just her style to shower the children—and adults—with her patient love, but she could have chosen to get pastries from one of the other stores or shops, or even purchased them out at the lodge.

Her act of kindness extended beyond a debt of gratitude she felt she owed Layton. She'd spread her joy to me and had taken some pressure off. That one sale—before I'd technically opened the doors—had been enough to ensure I'd be able to buy supplies to bake again tomorrow.

I crossed the dining room and cleaned up the booth where I had been eating, before retracing my steps back to the kitchen to help Isabel and Marcus with a second round of baking to restock my displays cases.

———

*I* really hadn't expected the summit to affect my business. If anything, I thought it might have been the reason I'd been slow over the past few days. The queen's event had done so much for the entire community, giving many temporary employment opportunities but taking them out of downtown and moving them to the lodge.

Today the opposite was true.

We had a steady traffic throughout the day and even needed to bake a third round of lemon tarts. Many of the customers mentioned they were summit attendees who had seen and smelled the pastries Mrs. Alscher had brought into the dining room that morning.

We'd been so busy, it took both Marcus and Isabel to fill orders, while I waited on customers and attempted to keep the dining area tidy. We were in a pre-lunch lull, and I took a moment to sit on one of the stools at the counter and give my feet a break.

Thirty seconds later, Isabel showed up with a cup of coffee for me. I could smell the dash of cinnamon before I realized she was standing in front of me. "I thought you could use it."

I gratefully accepted. "Thank you so much. You and Marcus should take your lunch while you can."

She gave me a brief nod. "We just took the bread out of

the oven. Marcus is making sandwiches for us now. You too. We've been so busy, you must be getting hungry."

I slid off the stool. "I am and would love to eat with both of you. Dad is out at the summit, and I don't think he will be coming in for lunch today."

I started to follow Isabel back to the kitchen when the bell over the door rang out, announcing another customer. "Go ahead and eat," I called after her. "I'll take care of the customer and be back in a few minutes."

I turned on my heel, surprised to see Layton approaching the counter. He was dressed in a tailored suit. It was a deep navy with a white dress shirt under the jacket and a brilliant light blue tie that emphasized the color of his eyes.

"I didn't expect to see you today."

He closed the distance between us and pulled me into a hug. A welcomed surprise, it awakened my desire for him, even though it never crossed the boundary of a friendly greeting.

Still, it sent a warmth radiating from my center. I held him close a few seconds longer than good manners would call for, but he didn't seem bothered. Instead, he held my gaze as he slowly slid back. "You are all I've been able to think about today."

"I've been thinking about you too." My cheeks warmed with the admittance.

Layton's picked at a stray curl that had fallen from my ponytail. "I had to come thank you for the perfect cup of coffee you sent up this morning."

"You're welcome, but you didn't have to drive all the way in to do that. I'm sure you're very busy."

"We have been this morning, but we're on a break now. You must be dead on your feet. I've kept you out so late last night."

"I'm a big girl. I made my own choices." Conversation ceased, and I found myself mesmerized in his presence.

As the silence grew uncomfortable, Layton slid up onto one of the stools at the counter. "If I'm going to stay awake through the afternoon sessions, I'm going to need another large cup of your special blend."

I turned toward my percolators to retrieve his order. "I'm sure they have coffee up at the lodge."

"Not nearly as good as yours. I have another request. Rather, this one comes from your queen."

He had my interest piqued now. What could the queen possibly want from me? "I don't understand."

"The sweet treats that Alma brought out for my children and some of the other guests caused quite the stir. It caught Queen Margaret's attention. Alma gave her one of your apple blossoms. She was just as mesmerized by them as everyone else. My children started raving about your cookies and hot chocolate."

"That's so kind of all of you."

"It's well deserved. Queen Margaret asked if you might consider bringing out cookies and hot chocolate for all the children for dessert tonight—just after the evening meal." He pulled a paper from the inside pocket of his jacket and unfolded it on the counter. "This is the order. She said if you bring an invoice with you this evening, she will pay for it immediately."

It was quite an honor, but I wasn't sure it was something I could even handle. I intently looked over the paper, wondering if I would have the time and supplies necessary. One cookie and one cup of hot chocolate for a hundred and fifty kids. A grand order, but manageable if Isabel and Marcus would work a bit of overtime. The profit from the order would be enough to easily pay them for the extra hours. "What time is dinner?"

"Six o'clock. Queen Margaret is speaking at seven-thirty, I think she hoped the staff would serve the children's desserts at that time."

"The Lodge is all right with serving my food?"

"The queen arranged everything. I told her you had a small staff, so she arranged for the Summit's staff to serve the desert. She would just need you to deliver it by seven o'clock. Can you handle the order?"

I briefly nodded, even though I was still rolling it over in my mind. "There is plenty of time to bake the cookies and prep the cocoa after I close the Bistro. And I do have some catering pans and carafes for transporting. I don't see any reason why I couldn't do it."

His smile widened. "Then you will?"

"Yes." I could give the royal family a price break for the large order and still make a nice profit. Having the queen's stamp of approval on my shop could only help business in the future. Right?

I owed all of this to Layton and Mrs. Alscher. I rounded the counter. This time I initiated the hug, wrapping my arms around his neck. He pulled me in tighter, holding me close. "If you can be there by six, I would be honored if you would have dinner at my table."

I pulled back, running my hands over my apron. "I appreciate the offer, but I'm not an attendee, and as a supplier—"

"Once you deliver the food and drink, your vendor role will be over. I would like you to be my guest and will arrange the formalities. Please say yes."

I couldn't refuse him after all he had done. I didn't *want* to. The idea of spending more time with Layton was making me lightheaded and weak in the knees. "Yes."

He pulled me close to him again and whispered in his ear. "Any time, *mano meilė*." He pulled away and reached for his wallet.

"Please. You've done so much. A cup of coffee is the least I can give."

He got a playful glint in his eyes. "Well, I'd also like a chocolate chip cannoli. How much is—"

"It's on me." I turned and went around the counter again.

"Oh, *mano meilė*, the images you put in my head."

My heart beat fast enough when we were together. If he continued to flirt, he would surely drive me mad. I wrapped the cannoli in a sheet of waxed paper and put it in a bag. Turning back, I handed it across the counter to him.

"Until tonight."

"I'll see you then."

On the street, he approached a waiting black sedan that I recognized as the one the queen and king had been ushered to the night before. As Layton advanced, a driver emerged and held the door for him.

I hadn't doubted the validity of Layton's tale, but seeing he had use of the Montgomery royal's car confirmed the details of his story.

*The queen had tasted my apple blossoms and requested I make dessert for all the kids.*

The weight of this began to sink in. Every single bite of cookie and every sip of cocoa would have to be perfect. A combination of rich and sweet. If I hit the mark, it could mean more requests from the royal family.

*This* could be the moment my business went from struggling to stable.

I turned to go tell Isabel and Marcus the good news, and found Isabel standing in front of me with the sandwich she mentioned before. "You really should eat."

"Thank you." I took the plate and took a bite, not realizing how starving I was until the mix of salami and mustard danced along my tongue, awakening my taste buds and hunger.

After swallowing I spoke. "I hope you and Marcus can stay late. I just got a big catering order. One hundred and fifty chocolate chip cookies and we'll have to fill all four of those large carafes with cocoa by five-thirty tonight."

The way her face lit up, I knew she'd been just as worried about our slump in sales. "That is wonderful. Of course, I will stay. I only hope we have enough flour and chocolate chips."

It was a valid concern. Our production just for the day had been more than double what we normally baked. "We better check it out."

After taking another bite of my sandwich, I followed her into the kitchen to take inventory of supplies.

# CHAPTER FOUR

*A*fter returning to the summit, Layton must have told the queen I accepted the order, because someone from her staff—Garan—called with very specific instructions on how and where to deliver the order. He gave me his number to call as soon as I arrived.

The lunch rush had been very busy and continued well into the afternoon. Again, it seemed summit attendees were sneaking away to have one-on-one conversations or just take a break from the swirl of activities at the lodge. Almost all ordered a dessert, proving I had Mrs. Alscher to thank for the sudden interest in my bistro.

Our supplies were running low, so I made out a list, and Isabel agreed to take some money from the register and do the shopping after we finished fulfilling the order for the summit. She'd deliver the supplies back to the bistro before going home for the night, so I would have a fully stocked kitchen to start the morning baking.

At the kitchen entrance to the Lodge, Garan found me. After getting the invoice, he directed me toward the lodge's contact person. That woman grabbed three other staffers, dressed in usual kitchen black and white clothes. They retrieved the trays and carafes from my car and disappeared.

I was about to search for a way to get to the main dining room—and look for Layton—when the assistant to the queen reappeared, handing me a check. I glanced at it to see they had got the amount wrong.

"I'm sorry, sir," I said, "but you've overpaid. I didn't bring change with me."

He smiled at me as if I had amused him. "Ma'am, it is a gratuity, authorized by the queen. She is very appreciative for your hard work to provide the special treats for the children. They all loved the ones at breakfast, and she is grateful for the chance to spread smiles to even more kids this evening. Now, if you will follow me, I can take you to his royal highness, Prince Layton. I know he anxiously awaits your arrival."

As I followed Garan through the kitchen, I became self-conscious of my appearance. Thanks to an obsessive concern of spilling flour on myself I did have a clean change of clothes in my office, but they were traditional restaurant wear—black pants and a white blouse—much like the Lodge's kitchen staff wore.

It may be true the prince wanted to spend time with me, but what would others think about him sitting with a woman who so obviously worked in a kitchen for a living?

Those who didn't know better might even think I worked here in the lodge and, for some audacious reason, had decided to sit down next to a prince.

I needn't have worried though.

It was as if Layton could feel my presence. I'd only covered half the distance of the dining room, when he looked up and caught my gaze. He smiled and excused himself from the conversation with his teenaged assistant, stood, and crossed to me. "Thank you, Garan, for showing Georgianne the way."

"My pleasure, sir."

Suddenly, I remembered the extra cookies. "I almost forgot. There are a dozen extra cookies, a thank you to the queen for the order. Can you please make sure she gets them?"

"Certainly, ma'am." With that, he walked away. I couldn't take my eyes off Layton, though. I steeled my stomach as he leaned in and wrapped his arms around my neck, kissing my cheek briefly. "I'm so glad to see you again. Thank you for coming."

"Are you kidding me?" I whispered in his ear. "Thank you for the large order."

He waved a hand in front of his face. "All I did is deliver a message for Queen Margaret." Layton took a step back but still held my hand, his gaze traveled down my body and back up again. "Simply stunning, *mano meilė*. Come sit."

Layton led me back to the table where he held my chair. It was only after I was seated I noticed all the eyes on me. It drove home why he'd insisted we have coffee and dessert away from the public dining room the previous evening. Having your every move under such scrutiny must be taxing. I wondered how Layton dealt with it as well as he appeared to.

He must have sensed my awareness, because he leaned over and whispered in my ear. "Never mind prying eyes. It is something I find nearly impossible to escape."

I smiled at him and slid the napkin from the table to my lap. It was only one meal. He lived with it daily, I could endure it for a couple of hours. It was the least I owed him after everything he had done for me.

He began introducing the children to me again, and each of them seemed excited that I was joining them. Each thanked me again for the cookies and cocoa the day before and seemed excited to be getting the same treat today.

All except Hannah used broken English. It seemed Layton or his assistant had been working with them.

Hannah gushed about the lemon tart she'd had for breakfast.

As I glance around the open dining room, I noticed Layton was in the minority. Most of the children seemed to be sitting with aides and chaperones while the actual summit attendees seemed to be congregated at tables together. I asked Layton why he wasn't sitting with his fellow attendees.

"I haven't been able to see my children all day." He paused for a quick beat. "I would much rather sit with them, and you, than anyone else."

I could feel my cheeks flush again and bowed my head to hide it. He must think me an adolescent the way he could make me blush with a kind word or a touch to my hand.

Either that—or a virgin—which I wasn't, by the way. Inexperienced, maybe. Virgin, no. "You must find me amusing then." Awkward, but I didn't know what else to say.

"Delightful." His crystal blue eyes bore into me.

If felt like he could see clear to my soul.

From the corner of my eye, I saw Mrs. Alscher enter the dining room. She scanned the crowd until her eyes settled on Layton and me. She waved in our direction, and I waved back.

She slowly maneuvered her way through the maze of people, stopping to speak to others with the ease and grace I notice in Layton the night before.

I saw a vibrancy in her I hadn't seen until she'd been reunited with her cousin. There was no doubt she was in her element, and must have missed being part of a larger community.

Eventually, she made it to the table and came up behind

Layton, squeezing his shoulders. "What a lovely day, Layton! I can't thank you enough for arranging this for me."

He stood, and spun to the woman. "My dear, Alma. This summit would not be the same without your wisdom and elegance.

"You are too kind." She stepped sideways and gave her attention to me. I stood to greet her.

She wrapped an arm around my neck, pulling me in and kissing my cheek. "My dear. You look lovely. How kind of you to make treats for all the children tonight."

"Please! Mrs. Alscher, I should thank you. I do believe you knew exactly what you were doing when you brought those pastries this morning."

She chuckled. "Are you accusing me of something?"

"Only of being the kindest woman I know. Isabel and Marcus owe you a debt of gratitude too."

She waved a hand in front of her face. "Nonsense. It was your delicious food that won over the queen. It had nothing to do with me."

The clatter in the dining room was lowering to a dull roar. I looked around and noticed everyone was finding their seats. The kitchen staff were wheeling out carts contain the dinner plates.

Mrs. Alscher squeezed my hand. "Enjoy your dinner, my dear. I see there is a seat right there next to Hannah. I can't wait to hear how she's enjoying the summit.

Even though I had no reason to believe she was insincere—and interested to hear from the kids—I had no doubt she was also giving Layton and me some privacy. She seemed to have it in her head that we would be a perfect couple.

While I was enjoying my time with him, it seemed any chance of even talking again after the week was over would be slim.

We were from two different worlds in every way that mattered.

Soon, it was our tables turn to be served. The children—well trained on proper manners from Layton—were respectful and impeccably behaved through the meal.

While we were eating, Layton took the time to ask each child pointed and appropriate questions about their day, drawing me into the conversation at every turn. It reminded me of family dinners when I was a child, and I could see that was the very same experience he was trying to give the orphans in his care.

As the meal was finishing up, the lights in the dining room dimmed and a spotlight hit the center of the stage. The queen stood at the podium and began her keynote address.

From the corner of my eye, I saw Layton press his finger to his lips, motioning for the children to be quiet. While he was as rigid and stern as he had been in the bistro the day before, this time I saw a kindness radiating in his eyes.

Something I hadn't noticed yesterday.

Instantly, they set their silverware down and folded their hands in their laps.

He always referred to the children as *his* and didn't act as an administrator. I now saw he acted as a parent. He was tough. He set down rules and expected the children to behave, but he did so with a great love. He didn't brush them aside to sit with chaperones.

They were with him.

*His.*

Layton's hand fell to a spot just above my knee. Instant warmth spread through me. I dropped my hand to rest on his, wanting to be more connected to this man. I was learning he was much more beautiful inside than he was on the outside. And his looks were damn fine too.

I tried to focus on what the queen was saying. She

personally welcomed those who'd travelled from near and far and spoke of the importance of the spirit of every human—of making them feel value and love—despite their circumstances. She held up Layton as an example of someone who put his heart into his work. Didn't treat it as a job, but gave of his soul to serve the needs of the children.

From the corner of my eye, I could see him lower his chin. His jaw set and his lips flattened. Clearly, he didn't like being singled out.

I squeezed his hand. I'd only known him a couple of days, and was already aware that this was how Layton lived his entire life. He'd displayed that unending wealth of kindness to me. In the two short days, I'd also learned he didn't like being singled out for it, either.

It was who he was and how he believed all people should be.

As the queen spoke, the lodge's wait staff began delivering the cookies and cocoa to the kids.

Around me I could hear rustling as the children began to enjoy the treats. Except for the ones sharing a table with us. They all eyed Layton cautiously.

He leaned over the table and spoke quietly. "Enjoy your desert, but show respect for the queen and do your best to be quiet." He then repeated the message—I assumed—in his native language.

The queen only spoke for about twenty minutes. Not so long that the children would become restless. As she finished, and the lights in the room came up, the room erupted in applause. Much of the crowd—Layton and I included—rose to our feet.

I turned to Layton. "Thank you for inviting me tonight. I'm so glad I was able to hear her speech."

"I wish she wouldn't have singled me out, everyone in this

45

room is working toward the same goal. However, she is a passionate speaker and a champion of the cause."

I was about to tell him he shouldn't be so modest, when Hannah came up to me, tugging on the ends of my blouse. "Thank you so much for the cookie and the cocoa."

"You're very welcome." I reached down and touched a stray curl framing her face. "But it is the queen who purchased the dessert for all of you."

"But you made them. Right?"

I nodded.

Layton squatted down so that he was at eye level with the young girl. "It was very polite of you to thank Georgianne. That makes me so very proud of you."

The girl smiled, seemingly pleased with herself and with Layton's praise.

Other children from the table followed in Hannah's footsteps and began to form a line to offer their thanks. I was overwhelmed by the outpouring. Part of me impressed with the impeccable manners and part of me saddened by the fact that, as orphans, the children had such little joy that a chocolate chip cookie meant so much.

After Delilah, the oldest—and the one serving as Layton's assistant—gave me her thanks, I turned back to Layton, to see the queen, accompanied by King Sinclair, had approached.

Seeing that I had finished with the children, Layton introduced me to Queen Margaret."

"It's a pleasure, your royal highness."

She took my hand and gave it a squeeze. "Thank you so much for baking such a large order on such short notice. To see the smiles on the children's faces, bring such joy to my heart."

"It was my pleasure."

"I almost hate to ask, but after the treats that Alma shared with some of the children this morning, I know they would all be disappointed if we don't have more tomorrow. Would it be possible for you to bake enough pastries to feed the summit tomorrow morning?"

I glanced around the room, trying to estimate a count, knowing in my heart I wouldn't refuse the queen. I couldn't turn down an order of that size. It would mean too much to my business and to Isabel and Marcus.

"I would be honored, ma'am."

"Georgianne," Mrs. Alscher interrupted. "Are you sure you can fill that order? They will need to be delivered very early."

"I can cook overnight and bring them out as early as you need them."

"And still work your bistro tomorrow?"

"I will find a way." I twisted on my heel, back to Queen Margaret. "Thank you so much for the invitation tonight, but I must get to work on this order."

Layton held a finger up, signaling for me to wait for him. He then walked around the table and whispered in Delilah's ear. He then paused, and spoke in a hushed voice to the queen and king.

I couldn't hear his words over the clatter of people exiting the dining room, but I was sure he was following some unbeknown royal protocol in saying goodnight. Once he'd finished the king and queen left, followed closely behind by their security detail.

Layton then came back to me, taking his hand. "I've made arrangements for Delilah to put the children to bed. Please, let me accompany you back to your bistro and help you with the queen's order."

I couldn't have heard him right? "Really, your royal highness? You want to spend the entire night in a hot kitchen baking."

The light in his eyes dimmed. He dropped his chin, and the corners of his mouth folded down.

I felt an immediate pang of guilt for wounding him. It hadn't been my intention. I had used his title in jest, not realizing how serious he'd been about trying to shake it off.

He quickly shook off the injury, though, and stepped closer to me, reaching for my hand, "I would love nothing more than to spend the evening with you, the task we share is of no consequence."

The words he chose were poetic. This—coupled with his mannerisms—was probably why most people, including me, found it hard to forget he was royal.

Truth was, knowing the days he would be in Montgomery were ticking away, I would love for him to spend the night with me.

I wasn't sure if cooking was my first choice of activity.

# CHAPTER FIVE

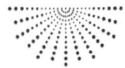

*B*ecause I would be returning to the lodge as soon as we were done baking, Layton rode with me to the bistro. He sat quietly in the passenger seat, looking out his window. His hands folded neatly on his lap. He seemed to be the perfect picture of peace and calm, but I got the feeling there was a storm of emotions raging beneath the surface.

I unlocked the back door to my café and held it for him.

I hung up my coat on the hook by the back door, and he shed the jacket to his suit, placing in on the hook next to mine.

He looked around the kitchen, taking in the boxes stacked on the metal prep tables.

"Oh good. It looks like Isabel picked up all of the supplies we'll need." I retrieved two aprons from where they hung inside the pantry and gave one to Layton, before putting the other on. I crossed to the boxes and unpacked the apples and lemons first. "I guess a good place to start would be peeling and chopping the apples for the blossoms and squeezing lemons for the tarts."

He picked up the bags of lemons and found a clean

surface, pulling a cutting board out from the lower shelf of the work station, and picking a knife from the block.

"There is a micro plane in the drawer near the stove. I need zest from the lemons as well."

"Is this a family recipe," he asked as he plucked a bowl from a hook above his head, and got to work slicing the lemons in half.

He still seemed miles and miles away, and I suspected something I said had changed his mood. I collected my own set of tools, and set up on the opposite side of the same prep table. As I began to peel the apples, I couldn't hold my tongue any longer. "You're being uncharacteristically quiet."

My comment lifted his spirits. "It pleases me you can already tell when I'm being moody."

"Did I upset you?"

"Not intentionally."

I felt my stomach drop. This man had been so kind. Intentional or not, it broke my heart that I had misspoke. "I'm sorry. Even though my mother worked in the palace, I really don't have that much experience with royalty. What did I do?"

His mouth curved downward again. "You have behaved most appropriately. You did not offend me."

"But I *did* say something wrong."

"Yesterday, it was so refreshing when you didn't know who I was."

From what I'd seen at the lodge, it seemed I was the only one who didn't identify Layton immediately. "I feel like an idiot for not recognizing you."

"I loved that you didn't. I appreciated your honesty in the way you treated me. Your skepticism. Your fear that I was too strict with the children. These are things I don't often see."

"You feel like people treat you differently because you're a prince?"

"I know they do."

I hadn't felt like I'd changed my behavior, but maybe he believed otherwise. "And I did too?"

"Oh, heavens no."

"Then I don't understand."

When I offered to help you this evening, you didn't believe I—as a prince—really wanted to be here."

She now remembered the joke she'd made, and the look on his face when she'd called him *his royal highness*. But…that *was* his title. "I'm sorry, Layton. I remember what you're talking about now. I was teasing, but I do find it hard to believe that *anyone* would want to spend the night baking."

Having finished squeezing the lemons, he'd retrieved the garbage can from the corner, and begun discarding of the peels, pulps, and seeds. "You enjoy it. Don't you?"

"I do, but it's my passion."

His eyes gleamed again. "I love to bake. I don't get to do it as often as I would like. It doesn't really matter that I'm sixth in line and will never sit a single day on the throne, I still have obligations to family and country that keep me very busy."

"It's a lot of pressure?"

"Mostly no, but sometimes—times like this—very much so."

"What is it about this summit?"

"It's *not* the summit, Georgianne. It's *you*." He walked around the prep table and stood in front of me. His hand going to the loose hair that had fallen out of my pony tail. "I don't know if you realize how absolutely smitten I've become with you."

My gut's first instinct was to look away and break eye contact with him. As much as I returned his desires, what would ever become of us? If the fact he was royalty and I was the owner of a barely-keeping-its-head-above-water bistro wasn't enough to separate us, miles upon miles did. When the summit ended on Friday, he would jet out of Montgomery, and I had too many obligations to be able to follow.

Still, I couldn't help but lean into his touch. My desire for him had been all-consuming.

He stepped even closer, wrapping his other hand around my waist. He dropped his mouth to mine, and I melted into his embrace.

Where all other physical contact between us could be described as cordial, Layton's kiss left no doubt as to how he felt about me. His fingers tangled in my hair while his tongue explored my mouth.

I pressed my hands to his back, pulling him tighter to me. I hoped it was clear I wanted this as much as he did.

When he pulled away, emptiness filled the space that had been bursting with desire. Goosebumps covered my flesh that had been warmed by his touch. I leaned forward, blatantly begging for another taste of him, instead he planted a soft kiss to my forehead. "We have so much work to do."

I dropped my chin and stepped back. "You're right."

His hand slid behind my neck, pulling me back into his personal bubble, "But when we have met your obligations, I want to pick up right where we left off."

I couldn't speak. Only nodded. Internally, I was condemning myself, making lists of all the reasons why kissing Prince Layton was the dumbest thing I'd ever done, but his touch had broken the dam holding back my raging desire. I'd wanted him, from the first moment he'd walked into my bistro. But I also knew when he returned to Ronaria my heart would break.

I saw no way we'd be able to bridge the gap distance and obligations would create.

It seemed ridiculous to even be thinking about a long-term future with Prince Layton only forty-eight hours after meeting him, but the mutual attraction between us burned so hot, never seeing him again left me aching.

He squeezed my hand tight. "Why don't I take over peeling and chopping these apples, while you teach me how to make that delightful lemon filling for the tarts.

I pushed up on my toes and left a chaste kiss on his lips. "To hold you over until later," I whispered. I then rounded the prep table and retrieved sugar from the boxes. From the refrigerator, I grabbed a large block of cream cheese.

Back at the table I dropped a couple of spoonsful of lemon juice on the apples before I began mixing the other ingredients into what remained.

"I feel like your sharing state secrets with me."

"Honestly, they are simple recipes."

"The best ones usually are."

He watched me mix ingredients, all the while peeling and dicing the apples. After a few minutes, he broke the silence. "Tell me more about yourself."

"There really isn't much to say. I had a normal upbringing. As you know, my father works with the foster care system, and at times we had foster children living in our home. My mother died a few years ago."

"I'm so sorry. Was she ill?"

I shook my head. Talking about it was still very hard. "It was a car accident. I was away at college. She was driving home from her job at the palace. There'd been a winter storm, and the roads were icy. She slid across the center line and was hit head on."

"How horrible. I'm so sorry."

I couldn't speak, only nodded, accepting his condolences.

"She worked for the royal family?"

"In their kitchen. She taught me her love of food and

putting care into preparing it. She always said food is more than nourishment. It should be enjoyed."

"She taught you well."

I managed a nod, afraid if I said anything more, I would begin to cry. I motioned to the bowl I was stirring. "This was her favorite desert, which is why there will always be lemon tarts available in here."

"You studied culinary arts, I assume." Having finished dicing the apples, Layton pushed the bowl aside.

I pulled it to me and began adding brown sugar and cinnamon and then mixed the ingredients. "I did, but not at first. I got an associate's degree in business before going on to culinary school."

"Did you have a different plan?"

I forced a smile to hide the pain behind my career shift. "I always wanted to do something like this but was afraid. I started business school because I wanted a degree that would give me something stable. I wanted good credentials to go work for someone else. After my mom's accident, I realized how short life can be. In an instant, everything can be pulled out from under you. I was in my freshman year and knew immediately I needed to follow my dream. I'm not much for quitting, however. I met with my academic advisor, changed up my plan to get an associate degree in business instead of a bachelor. While working on that degree, I started refining my skills and got a job in a restaurant near the school to increase my chances of getting into the culinary school."

"Your amazing. You see something you want and you just go after it, full force."

"Make a plan, make it happen." When Layton looked at me with question, I explained, "My father's favorite words of advice. They've served him well, and me too"

"I have a lot of respect for your father. He has a well-run program here."

"He is a good man."

"As is his daughter."

Looking across the table, into Layton's gaze, I saw a smoldering heat that appeared to be growing the longer we spent time together.

Pushing aside the seasoned apples, I collected what was needed to make the base for my lemon tarts, and then turned the spotlight to the Prince. "How about you? Tell me about your life."

"I promise it's not as interesting as yours."

"You've probably done more and seen more than I could ever hope to."

"Ronaria is a very small, very poor country. My family does well, but we do not spend lavishly. We feel it's more important to take care of our people. We put the needs of our nation above our personal desires."

"But you were able to come to this summit and bring some of the children."

"If not for the fact your queen wanted my children here, I wouldn't have come."

"But it's a passion of yours."

He nodded. "I couldn't justify spending the money when we have so many in need, but Margaret is offering some special grants to the nations who came to the summit that would greatly help my program and my children. It took some convincing from me, but Father decided it was worthy enough to send us."

"From what I can tell, when you want something, you get it."

Under my direction, he began pressing the shortbread dough into the bottom of the muffin tins to make the base for the tarts, while I started mixing the dough for the apple blossoms.

"When I feel passionate about something, I do everything

in my power to make it happen."

"Like convincing Queen Margaret to place these large orders?"

"I had very little to do with that."

I put my hands on my waist and gave him my *I don't believe you* look.

"It happened just as I said." He chuckled. "Alma is also very persuasive. I learned today she is quite fond of you."

"Mrs. Alscher is wonderful. She's been so good to me from the moment I opened the doors. How is it she's your cousin but lives so far from your family."

Confusion tipped his mouth. "Really? You don't know."

"I guess I don't."

"Twenty years ago, she was next in line to reign. In fact, she did my very job. On a trip to Montgomery, she met Roan Alscher. They fell in love, and she relinquished her position in line to rule so that she could come here and marry him. She was an only child, and when her father died, the throne passed to my father."

"I had no idea." But, as I looked back it became clear she and Layton were a lot alike. She acted as kind, generous, and royal as he did. "Giving up her throne seems like a great sacrifice. Why would she do that?"

His mouth curled up into a sinful smile. "For love, of course."

"But…a nation depended on her."

"You would rather have her sacrifice her own heart?"

"Of course not." That wasn't Alma's way. She'd embraced me and my goals the moment I'd opened the door to the bistro. She'd been my very first customer and had graced the steps of the shop daily. "She couldn't have both? Why not?"

"Nothing prevented her from marrying Roan and becoming queen, but it was a different world then. He had family and work here. Travelling between our nations wasn't as easy as it is now. It wasn't practical."

That made a lot of sense. Even though two decades had passed, and the chances Layton would ever become King of his nation were slim, I felt like distance and responsibilities were enough to come between us. "I wish I would have known her husband. He must have been an incredible man for her to leave behind everything she knew and everyone she loved and move to a new country."

"We weren't on another planet. We—her family—weren't as close as we'd like to have been, but we'd see her—and Roan, when he was still alive—as much as we can." He paused from both speaking and the task at hand, and stepped away from the table. "He *was* an exceptional man. Roan and Alma were destined to be."

He leaned up against the refrigerator. The look on his face told me he was lost in a tangle of thoughts. Though a piece of me feared what he might be thinking, I couldn't stop myself from asking. "Is there something wrong?"

He shook his head, and walked back to the prep table. "What do you need me to do next."

"Those pans can go in the oven, set the temperature to three hundred and fifty and the timer for ten minutes."

He did as I asked and then slipped up behind me, watching over my shoulder as I rolled out the dough I'd just made.

His breath was hot on my neck, making my stomach light and my knees weak. I wanted to brace my hands on the edge of the table, sure the floor was going to spin out from under me.

Instead I tried to focus on the baking and picked up the bowl of apple and spices dumping them onto the dough. I spread it out and began to roll the mixture into a cylinder shape.

An arm came around my waist, he pressed his body against mine and his mouth hovered just inches from the crook where my neck met my shoulder. "Is this okay, Georgianne?"

I closed my eyes, trying to find the words, but the heat of him had evaporated my ability to speak.

"Please...I need just a taste. May I?"

Such chivalry. How he could be so close and not surrender to the passion that had been boiling between us I'll never know. But, he would have remained frozen in place for as long as it would have taken for me to grant permission. And if I'd denied him, I have no question he would have stepped back.

But denying Layton's kiss proved impossible.

"Please." My words sounded horse and frail. "I want you to."

I felt the hot breath he'd been holding caress my neck before his lips did. He slid his tongue against my pulse, driving it to raise as he caressed my stomach.

I laid my hands on his and leaned my body into him.

He moved his left hand to the other side of my neck sliding it up to my hair, where his fingers expertly pulled the tie away, letting my locks fall around my shoulders.

Not able to take it anymore, I turned his arms and captured his mouth with my own. I used the weight of my body to push us a few steps from the prep table. "Not... sanitary... to... have... my... hair... down," I mumbled between exquisite tastes of my prince.

He pulled his mouth away, but pressed his forehead to mine. His deep, throaty chuckle struck my core, churning my lust. "Really? That's what you're thinking about right now?"

I snaked my arms around his neck and kissed the dimple in his chin. "The teachers at culinary school scarred me with their incessive reminders."

His soft, supple lips pressed to mine again, and my body melted into him. His fingers danced against my spine, and his hip pressed to mine. "What you've done to me these last forty-eight hours."

I looked into his eyes and saw the same longing that burned inside me. "I haven't been able to think of much else except you since you came into my bistro." A realization hit me. "Did Mrs. Alscher tell you to meet her here?"

He slid his hand against my cheek and nibbled at my lower lip. "No. That was a happy coincidence."

I returned his kiss, and he deepened his advances. He clutched me tighter, pulling my hips tighter to his lean, firm body.

*What am I doing?*

Suddenly, I was bombarded with a range of emotions and thoughts. As much as I would love to push my dough and apples aside and let Layton hoist me up onto the prep table, it would be to what end? When the summit ended, he would take his lovely children back to Ronaria. He'd go back to being a prince in his nation, and I would remain here in my coffee shop. The business I'd so desperately wanted. My homage to everything my mother was.

What we were doing was crazy.

And stood in the way of fulfilling my commitment to the queen.

I pressed my hands against his shoulders and gently eased out of his grasp.

"Is something wrong?" Concern etched his features, and his hand reached for mine.

I clutched it and forced a smile. "I made a promise, and as delightful of a distraction that you are, I'm a woman of my word. I need to finish this baking."

He pulled on the tie of the apron, straightening it. "You're right. And I promised to help you."

## CHAPTER SIX

*A*fter our passionate distraction, Layton fell back into his prim and proper princely mode. He acted as a sous chef and served as my right hand, mixing batters, chopping ingredients, and helping the process move along. By four in the morning, we'd finished the order for the summit and stacked my display case with enough sweet treats to get Isabel and Marcus through until midday.

While Layton loaded the boxes into my SUV, I wrote up a list of instructions for the two of them, explaining that after I delivered the order to the lodge, I was going to go home and sleep for a few hours. I planned to be in before the lunch rush.

I heard Layton come back into the kitchen, his shoes clacking against the polished concrete floor as he closed the distance between us. His arms wrapped around my waist, and his mouth was on my neck again.

"Layton." I wiggled in his embrace.

"Your obligations to country and queen are fulfilled."

I slid my hand over my head, and tangled my fingers in his hair. "Not until the order is delivered."

"We have some time."

I spun in his arms, and accepted his sweet kiss to my mouth. "You need to rest."

"I'm not tired."

"You must be."

He shrugged. "I suppose I should try to grab a couple hours of sleep before my children rise. And a shower would probably be a good idea since I'm to speak to the entire summit during the breakfast session."

"I didn't know that. And you stayed up all night helping me?"

"I will be fine. After my speech, I can slip away and take a nap."

I pushed up on my toes, giving his mouth a quick peck. "We both need sleep. Let me get you back to the lodge."

He gave a curt nod. "It's unprincely of me, but I don't suppose I can convince you to sleep in my room?"

"Why do I feel like there wouldn't be much sleep going on."

He lifted his eyebrows in a sultry tease. "I wonder…"

I laid my head against his shoulder, and he kissed the top of my head. My heart was walking a dangerous path, falling deeply, madly in love with a prince who would never be mine.

———

*I* dropped Layton at the front door of the Lodge. It was closer to the elevators and his room. He kissed my cheek and made me promise to join him and his children for dinner again. I agreed, wondering if Alma would be there. I wanted to talk to her more about the history lesson Layton had shared with me.

I drove around to the back of the lodge and knocked at the steel, kitchen door.

Within moments, it opened, and I was greeted by a tall man wearing a uniform indicated he was the Lodge's Executive Chef. He didn't look pleased to see me.

"I have the pastry order for Queen Margaret."

He stepped aside. "You can bring the boxes is in and stack them on the cart just inside the door."

It was a three-sixty reaction to how I'd been greeted by the queen's staff the day before, but I understood the chef's apprehension. I would feel put out if a customer had requested another chef bring their food to my bistro.

I was also quite aware that, as much as he might want to sabotage my efforts and serve his own pastries, he wouldn't dishonor the queen by lying. I could be sure my order would be delivered.

Still, I would shoot off a text to Garan when I left, just to be sure.

I decided to not make any waves and did as he asked. I brought the boxes in and stacked them neatly on the tray.

On the top of the stack, I positioned the small box with the lemon tart for the queen and attached the tag bearing her name.

I looked over the invoice, which included my mailing address and phone number, and left it between the top large box and the special treat for her royal highness.

I inched my way into the kitchen and found the man who'd greeted me at the door. I said a polite thank you and goodbye to the executive chef. He gave me a slight smile, demonstrating that as bruised as his ego was over the situation, he wasn't going to hold me personally responsible.

I started for the door I'd entered through but hesitated. The desire to go to Layton's room came over me. It felt wrong to leave without saying goodbye.

*Yeah, we'll say* that *is why I wanted to go to his room.*

But my mind took over for my heart and pushed my feet to take the most direct path to my car. Behind the steering wheel, I sent a quick text to the queen's right-hand man, letting him know I'd made the delivery and informed him where I'd left the invoice. It was only five, so I was surprised when he almost immediately responded with *Thank you. The queen will be pleased. You will have your payment by the end of the day.*

I started the car and eased the transmission into drive, pointing myself toward home.

I thought about how the two nice paychecks from the castle would help me get ahead at the bistro but wondered how long the financial cushion would last. The queen might enjoy my mother's lemon tarts, but would she need large orders of them once the summit was over?

Thinking about after the summit made my heart ache.

How had I become so accustomed to Layton in such a short time? I would miss him terribly when he returned to his homeland.

I walked into the house and entertained the idea of showering, getting dressed, and heading into work.

Isabel and Marcus had so little experience opening, maybe it was smarter to work the morning and come home early. Isabel could certainly handle closing.

I shook the notion off. It might be a smarter plan, but there was no way I could go into work now. I'd been up for more than twenty-four hours and was fading fast.

A few hours of sleep was the first order of business.

I was halfway up the staircase, when I saw my father working his way down.

"Did you forget something this morning?"

Did he think I'd been home and had gone to work already? I briefly wondered if the truth was the best response here, but quickly decided it was the only way to answer. "No. I'm just getting home."

His eyes widened. "You spent all night with Prince Layton?"

"Yes, but it's not what you think. The queen placed another order. For breakfast pastries this time. Layton came into town and helped bake them."

"Layton."

There was no emotion in the way he said the prince's name. I searched my mind for the reason he was displeased and landed on the fact I hadn't added his title to his name. "He asked me to forgo formalities."

"He did?" My father paused. I'd never really seen him at a loss for words. For the first time in my life, I wondered what was going on in his mind.

"It was kind of him to give up his night to help you. He is supposed to speak this morning, you know."

"I didn't until he told me about an hour ago. He says he will be fine, but had I known, I would have insisted on filling the order on my own."

Father nodded. "My understanding is the young prince is accustomed to things going his way. I have a feeling if he wanted to help you, you would have eventually seen eye-to-eye with him."

I knew, from personal experience, my father was right, but there was no need to say so. There was also no reason to tell Dad, I'd also been mouth to mouth with Layton. He seemed uncomfortable with just the idea of me spending time with the prince. I wasn't sure how he would react to know something—whatever it was—was blossoming between us.

"I left Isabel and Marcus a note explaining the situation and let them know I would be in by eleven—in time to set up for lunch. I'm going to grab a few hours' sleep and get a shower."

"It's good that you have people you can rely on. When you're done for the day, come home and get some rest." He passed me and continued down the stairs.

I considered withholding the fact I had plans with Layton but knew he'd see me with him in the Lodge's dining hall later and wonder why I had kept the details to myself. "Layton has asked me to dine with him again tonight. I suppose I will see you at the summit."

I figured the news would stop him in his tracks again, but he barely broke his stride. Looking over at his shoulder, he gave me a confused nod. Apparently, he wasn't sure what to make of his daughter dating a prince.

Truth be told, neither did I.

# CHAPTER SEVEN

*A*fter catching a few hours of sleep, I'd showered and dressed. My chosen attire wasn't what I'd normally wear to work. I dressed for the evening ahead of me, bringing a fresh apron from home to help keep my clothes clean.

Isabel showered me with questions the moment I arrived and when she'd learned I was headed back to the summit after we closed the shop, she insisted I stay out front and leave the day's baking to her.

Though tired, the financial weight that had been lifted from my shoulders made it easy to greet customers and cheerfully serve them.

Again, many of the guests from the lodge took time away from the summit to come into my bistro, telling me the treats served had piqued their hunger and curiosity about my shop.

The buzz around the small town, had drawn in locals too. The lunch rush receipts were even better than the day before.

As the bistro began to quiet, I tasked Isabel and Marcus

with prepping the doughs and batters for the next day's baking while I counted down the drawer.

As busy as we had been, I was shocked we were all done cleaning up and prepping the next day, just as the clock was ticking to three.

Having finished arranging the deposit for the bank, I was about to cross the dining room to lock the front door, when I saw my father approaching with Layton and Mrs. Alscher.

I held the door for them. "I'm surprised to see you. I thought you would be eating up at the summit."

"We did," my father replied.

Layton paused in front of me, leaning in to kiss my cheek. "I wanted a quiet place—that served the best cappuccino I've ever tasted—to discuss a private matter with your father and my cousin. We're not too late, are we?"

I let my hand fall to his hip, holding him close for a moment longer than was appropriate for the length of time we'd known each other. "Of course, how could I refuse any of you? Caramel?" I now knew that to be a weakness for him.

"Please."

"Dad, Mrs. Alscher, what can I get you?""

"Just coffee for me," my father answered.

"The same for me. Here, let me help you?" Mrs. Alscher said.

I waved her off. "You're being ridiculous. No one in my bistro serves themselves. It will take just a few minutes to brew a fresh pot of coffee.

Behind the counter, I started the machine and then went into the kitchen, letting Isabel and Marcus go home.

"Are you sure," Marcus asked. "We can stay to help with this late table."

"It's not necessary. They've only ordered coffee, and I'm sure they won't be here long. They'll have to return to the summit soon."

"I know you had a long night," Isabel said.

"And the two of you must be bone-tired from the long few days we've had. Go home, I can take care of this table."

After my employees had left, I locked the back door and went to the display racks picking out an assortment of the pastries that were left. The choices were few, but they still looked desirable and I was confident they would taste fresh.

I set the small plate on a serving tray and prepped the two cups of coffee and Layton's cappuccino, before lifting the tray and carrying it to the table.

"It's not a small favor I ask," Layton said to my father. "But, I think it would be a good experience for both of us."

I looked at my father out of the corner of my eye. He looked very conflicted and immediately picked up the cup I set in front of him. "I never expected anything like this. It's not a decision I would take lightly or can make on the spot. There is so much to consider."

"I don't know what I'm going to do with you, Georgianne. If you keep feeding me these sweets, I'm going to need a new wardrobe," Mrs. Alscher said.

I couldn't stop smiling at the woman. Yes, I had been feeding her more treats than normal, but her svelte frame seemed none the worse for it. "Life is too short to not stop and taste the chocolate now and again."

She lifted one of Mom's lemon tarts from the platter. "Or lemon as it might be."

"Of course." I was grateful to have been drawn into the conversation but could tell, by the way Layton and Dad's gazes were locked on each other, they were holding their tongue while I hovered.

Layton placed his hand on the wide cup I'd set in front of him. "Thank you, Georgie." He brought it to his lips and took a sip. His eyes drifting shut, a pleasure filled smile tipping his lips.

"If you need anything else, let me know."

I retreated behind the counter, pushed the clean button on the cappuccino machine, and retrieved the pieces to the coffee pot. Taking them back into the kitchen. While I washed them, my thoughts drifted to the pieces of conversation I'd overheard. What type of favor could Layton be asking of my father? What did the two of them have in common.

*Their work and me.*

Certainly, he couldn't be asking for something about me. Maybe he was disciplined and mannered, but he had to know I was a modern woman who'd built her own business—I didn't need Daddy's permission for anything. Besides, it was ridiculous to think Layton would be having *that* conversation with my father after only a few days.

That only left work.

My confusion spiked higher. I went to the window between the kitchen and the dining room and watched them. Both leaned over the table, speaking quietly and intently.

I could make out nothing.

After a few minutes, Layton looked at his watch and then found his feet. "Where does the time go? I need to get back to the Lodge. I have a meeting with your queen in thirty minutes."

Dad and Mrs. Alscher stood. My father called out my name, and I went back into the dining room to say my goodbyes.

My father hugged my neck, a bit unusual, but not totally unheard of. His eyes showed his distraction. Whatever it was Layton had discussed with him was weighing heavy. "I'll see you this evening, sweetheart."

"Yes, of course."

My eyes met Layton's. And a smile lit up his face. "I'll meet you in the dining room right before dinner?"

"I'm looking forward to it."

———

*A*fter closing my bistro, I headed up to the lodge, hours before dinner. I could have used the extra time to take a nap or do some ordering for the store. Instead, I just wanted to get close to Layton, even if I wouldn't be able to see him until dinner.

I'd be lying if I didn't say my curiosity over Dad and Layton's coffee break wasn't weighing heavy on my mind, but I'd been able to explain it by the fact they worked in the same field with the same level of passion and dedication. Certainly, whatever they had to discuss it had been about work.

No matter how hard I tried to focus on my cafe, my mind kept spinning in the same tracks—each minute that ticked away was one closer to Layton's departure.

I blinked hard to push back the tears rimming my eyes.

*Don't be silly. What fun you've had, but he's a prince with a country to get back to you, and you are a barista who happens to own her bistro.*

In the lobby of the lodge, I unwrapped the scarf from my neck and took in the hustle and bustle. Groups of children played in every corner of the big open room while various chaperones kept a watchful eye. Except for Layton's children, the prince sat in a large red chair near the fireplace, watching the kids play.

He looked tired but very happy.

I hadn't expected to see him; I was sure he'd be in sessions right up until dinner time.

My heart beat wildly, and I felt sweat wetting my palms.

As if he could feel my eyes on him, he looked up and caught my gaze. His face brightened even more, and he maneuvered through the maze of children between the two of us.

When I was close, he wrapped an arm around my shoulder and kissed my cheek. "You're early. What an unexpected, yet joyous surprise."

I returned his hug and felt my knees weaken when his lips touched my flesh. "After closing the bistro, I wasn't sure what to do with myself. I was also curious to know if the queen was happy with the pastries this morning."

He motioned for me to sit in the chair next to the one he'd been in, and only after I sat, retook his seat. "I met with her not long ago, and she told me she was thrilled with what you had done. I do believe she'll speak with you at dinner."

I felt a heat rush to my cheeks. "I'm not used to all this attention."

"I think maybe it's something you should grow accustomed to."

I shrugged. "I don't know. The summit ends tomorrow. I imagine things will go back to normal then."

"Now that everyone knows about your food and coffee, I don't think you'll be slipping back into obscurity."

"I can only hope you're right."

His smile widened, and his stare deepened.

I must admit, I felt a little self-conscious under his adoring gaze but could almost hear cracking and sizzling from the sexual tension that continued to burn between us.

"I had hoped we'd have some time before dinner to talk." Layton scratched his temple, and his eyes searched the open room. "I'm sure you're curious about the conversation I had with your father."

I could do nothing more than nod, finding it hard to land on the words to express my twisted emotions.

He motioned for me to wait where I was seated for a

moment. "Let me grab Delilah to watch the children so we can go somewhere private to speak."

*Private.* Obviously, he never meant to keep whatever was being discussed from me, or he wouldn't have held the conversation in my bistro, but it did appear it was something he wasn't ready to share with anyone outside of a small circle of people yet.

After a few moments, Layton returned with his young assistant. He took my hand and helped me stand, leading me down a hall that ran off the front desk to what appeared to be the offices for the staff of the Lodge.

It felt wrong to me, like we'd crossed into an area reserved for officials and higher-ups. "Are we supposed to be back here?"

Layton chuckled. "It's fine. The staff has kindly given me use of one of the office spaces so that I can conduct my business with privacy."

At the end of the hall, he opened the door to a secluded room with no windows. Despite the lack of natural light, it was still warmly decorated.

There was a large desk but also a small loveseat, and a table with a coffee maker and an assortment of snacks. The treats had appeared to go untouched. He motioned for me to take a seat on the small couch and then dropped down next to me, gently placing a hand on my knee. "I'm not really sure where to begin, so I'm just going to spit this out. Surely, it will not be one of my more elegant speeches."

His words and nervousness widened my smile. Layton seemed to have both articulateness and confidence bred into him. If anything, I knew he would communicate whatever seemed to be tangled inside of him well, but the fact he was anxious about it gave him a vulnerability I hadn't seen before. If possible, I found him even more endearing.

"Georgianne, the moment I walked into your coffee shop,

you stole my heart. I know the idea of love at first sight seems ridiculous. It sounds outlandish to me. I've never been quick to my emotions and my priority—from the time I began public service—has always been my children."

He didn't need to tell me what the kids meant to him. His actions spoke volumes. "I admit you've made me feel things I'm not used to either."

"The idea of going home in a couple of days is not something I'm ready for. I can't imagine not being able to see you, to continue exploring what's going on between us."

I dug deep for the strength to admit my vulnerability. "I've been thinking a lot about you leaving too."

"I talked to your queen this morning and then, as you know, met with your father. I have an idea that they both seem quite interested in. I've proposed an exchange between our nations. I would come here and work in your father's office for the next six months, and he would go take my place in Ronaria."

As wonderful as it would be to have Layton here in town longer, the idea of not seeing my dad for so long twisted my stomach into knots. "You asked my father to move thousands of miles away?"

"For six months," he explained again, as if the short duration made it tolerable. He squeezed my hand. "It may seem drastic, but it was the only solution I could come up with. If your father and I make this exchange, it will give you and me the time to figure out this thing between us."

*This thing.* It seemed an odd choice of words for Layton, he'd always been so well spoken, but I understood it. If asked to describe the bubbling of emotions and raging attraction between us, I couldn't find the proper words either.

But...was sending my father out of the country a good solution.

"What did my father say?"

"That he needed some time to think about it. I assumed he wanted to consult you too." He laid a hand on my knee. "Georgianne, I thought you would be happy about this."

"I love the part about you staying, but does my father have to move thousands of miles away for us to be together?"

I hated the expression on his face, like he'd lost his best friend.

"I would worry about him."

The poignancy lifted from Layton's face. "He is a grown man, you know."

"Who was devastated after my mother's accident. We both miss her terribly. I'm not sure how he would handle being in a foreign land so far away from everyone he knows."

Layton's eyebrows scrunched together. "It is a good opportunity for him. My program is well respected."

"As is my father's. He's very good at his job."

"Of course, he is. I wouldn't have invited him to do this exchange if I didn't recognize that and respect both him and his work. We are talking about *my* children, after all. I wouldn't leave them in just anyone's care, but it's a sacrifice I'm willing to make."

In the shock of potentially missing my father, I had failed to realize what Layton would be giving up. His work meant the world to him. The way he felt for the children in his care was more than obvious to even the casual observer. And he was willing to do this to see if the incredible spark that happened between us could become a lasting flame. "I feel like it is too much for you to sacrifice."

"It's worth it to me to give us a fair shot."

*Us.*

A man I knew for only a few days was willing to leave everything he knew just because we had shared some laughs, smiles, and a couple of incredible kisses. I slid away from him and stood. "Layton. This is all a little overwhelming."

He came up behind me and rested his hands on my shoulder. "I realize this. If I had the time to go slow with you, I would, but it is ticking away. Don't you want me to stay?"

The pain in his voice ripped through my chest. My body acquiesced to his. There was no question I wanted more time with him. "Is it really that simple? What about your family and your responsibilities?"

"The distance will be hard, but we have the means to travel back and forth. I'm not turning my back on my responsibility to my country. I've arranged someone to fill in for me, and in the meantime, I will be learning from the resources of your nation."

I turned back to face him. "Can you really take a six-month sabbatical from being a prince?"

He tipped his chin and rubbed the back of his neck. "Even royalty deserve a holiday now and again. Don't you agree?"

"I feel like it's unfair for me to want you to stay. It's too much to ask you to leave your children and your people."

"You didn't ask."

"What happens at the end of six month? You'll have to go home sometime."

"Unless I decide to make one with you."

"And…what? Abandon your family, your duties?"

He laughed, shaking his head. "I'm sorry. It's not funny. But I am not like Alma. I have five elder brothers. It would take a natural disaster to put me on the throne."

A shiver climbed my spine. "Don't say such a thing."

He reached for my arm. "I didn't wish it. It's simply a fact. One I'm quite fine with. I will not lead. Still, I know my country depends on me to fulfill certain roles. To represent them to the world. I would never shirk those responsibilities."

I'd seen all I needed to in the last few days to know his character. A royal holiday was one thing, but he would eventually go home. Could I leave everything I had built here to follow him? Were we begging for more pain by trying to steal a little pleasure now? "I don't know if this is the smart thing to do."

Layton's hand slid from my arm and he stepped backward. "If it's not what you want, I will rescind my offer to your father."

"I don't know. I need time to think."

"We don't have a lot of time. The summit ends tomorrow."

# CHAPTER EIGHT

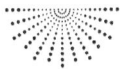

*I*t wasn't easy to walk away from Layton, but I needed to be alone to try and process everything he'd said to me. I didn't know what to think about the offer he'd made my father without talking to Dad, and I couldn't do that at the lodge with everyone's eyes on us.

I knew Layton valued his privacy too much. He wouldn't want anyone to know about the proposal until it was a certainty.

Probably why he'd come to my bistro to talk to my father.

So, I'd walked out of Layton's make-shift office and the lodge, got in my car, and drove home. Forgoing what might have been a last night with Layton, so I could decide if I could risk my heart.

I pulled the blanket tighter around myself and sipped from the cup of cocoa I'd made. The television was on, but I wasn't listening to it. All I could think about was the sacrifices Layton was willing to make, and my fear that, in the end, all we would gain from more time together was more pain when he eventually went home.

I was entwined in my thoughts. I hadn't heard the back-door slam nor realized my father was home until he sat down on the couch next to me.

"I'm surprised you're still up. You leave so early for the shop."

I forced a smile. "I have a lot on my mind."

"Layton said he'd told you about the offer he made me. I think it hurt him that you weren't happy about it."

"The last thing I wanted to do was seem ungrateful. The idea of him staying makes me happy. I just worry about how everyone else will suffer so that we can spend time together."

"You don't want me to go."

I shrugged and pulled the blanket a little tighter. "You do? We've leaned so heavily on each other since we lost Mom."

He nodded. "That's true. But we're both capable adults. The opportunity Layton is offering is generous. I'd get to work with new people, in a well-respected program, and learn other approaches."

"Layton said it would be a good learning experience for him too."

"I believe he's right, but if you want me to stay, I will."

"I don't want you to give up the opportunity."

He pinched my chin. "Then why the frown?"

"He thinks stepping away from everything he knows is worth it, but what if it isn't? What if he ends up resenting me? What if we grow close and both end up hurt worse when he must go home and I can't follow?"

Dad laid a finger against my mouth. "Taking a leap in hopes of finding love is worth the risk of getting hurt."

"I don't leap."

"What about opening your own bistro? That was an incredibly brave example of blind faith."

"And until this week, I thought I might fail. Success still isn't a certainty."

"It never is, Georgianne. That's the thing about taking

chances. Things might not work out. In my experience, you're never worse off for trying. If nothing else, you walk away with a lesson learned. However, you can't reach new heights without taking those first steps. My understanding is Layton isn't asking you for much, just to give him a chance."

"But what about all he's leaving behind? It's all too much to risk."

"He doesn't think so." Dad tapped my knee and then stood. "I'm headed to bed. You should too. Three o'clock will be here before you know it."

"Are you going to take Layton's offer?"

He looked back over his shoulder. "I'd like to. But if you'd rather I didn't, I won't."

"You deserve some happiness, and if this will give you that, I'd never stand in your way. I'll miss you, though."

He twisted on his heel and retraced his steps until he was standing in front of me. "It's a short distance and will only last for a minute in time."

"I know."

"What about you? Are you going to accept Layton's offer?"

"I don't know."

"That poor boy was in absolute agony tonight without you by his side. No matter your decision, don't keep him on the hook too long."

"I won't."

---

*F*ather was right about three in the morning. Sleep had been minimal, and I worked my way through my morning set ups in as if I were walking through a dream. Every corner of my kitchen bore a memory of Layton and I working on the queen's order together.

*Is that what it would be like if we pursued a relationship?*

*Would he help me cook?*

*Would he always make me smile with the same ease?*

*Would we learn we had nothing but this physical attraction between us and grow apart?*

I tried to shake off the negatives. What did we have to lose besides six months? If I had learned nothing else from my mother's death, it was that time sometimes meant all the difference.

*What would happen with Layton's children and his family while he was away?*

*Would he regret not being there to watch Steven grow or help Hannah adjust to her next phase of life.*

*What about Delilah? Layton depended on her to help him with the younger children, but I suspect she depended on him to be there for her too.*

Instead, my father would be there with Layton's children, presumably in close contact. Would Dad be able to connect with Layton's children and staff the way he seemed to?

Isabel and Marcus showed up on time, clocked in and went to work. Both tried to make small talk but seemed to read my mood with ease and respected my silent request to be with just the thoughts in my head.

Just a few minutes after unlocking the front door, Alma Alscher came in. She was dressed—again—in professional wear, a bright colored scarf covering her perfectly coifed hair.

"What can I get for you this morning?"

"I want a half dozen apple blossoms, a half dozen lemon tarts, and a cappuccino for my cousin, but first, I would like you to pour us both a cup of coffee and join me at a table so we can chat."

My chest heaved with a sigh. "I don't know what to say…"

"Then you can sit and listen to me." With that declaration,

she turned and glided across the room, with all the poise I'd known her to have but with a new sense of purpose. She pulled the scarf from her head as she went to her favorite booth and slid in.

After all she'd done for me, I couldn't deny Mrs. Alscher the conversation she requested. I poured two cups of coffee, preparing Alma's to her liking, and after calling Isabel to fill her to-go order, I crossed the restaurant and slid into the booth.

"What is it you're so afraid of?"

"Is that what Layton thinks?"

"Layton doesn't know what to believe. He fears maybe you don't feel for him the way he does for you."

I let out an exhale. "This has all happened so fast. My head is spinning. I've only known him a few days. It feels way too soon—way too crazy—for him to give up his life as he knows it."

Alma smiled warmly. "Layton doesn't give up much. This decision is something he sees as a win for all parties involved."

"He told me the day we met he sometimes wishes he could have a single day when he didn't have to be royalty. Maybe that's what he wants more than spending time with me?" I really hadn't realized the fear until I said it out loud. Maybe the reason I was resisting Layton was I had a hard time accepting his affection for me.

"You think he's turning his back on his country? An exchange like the one he is proposing with your father will benefit both of our nations. Travel is part of his everyday life."

"But he can't stay forever. If this is to work between us, won't one of us have to give up something important."

"Maybe."

"Did you ever regret leaving Ronaria for your husband?"

"Not for a single moment."

I slid my finger around the rim of the coffee cup. "I find that hard to believe."

"There were days I missed my family and my home. It took time to adjust to living here in Montgomery, but nothing that matters comes easy, and being with my Roan made it all worth it." She reached across the table and tapped my hand. "I see Isabel has my order ready. I need to get out to the summit. It's the last day, you know."

I nodded.

"If Layton doesn't hear from you today, I suspect he will rescind his offer to your father fly home with the children tomorrow."

I watched as she paid for her order and left my bistro, absorbing the words she said. She was right. I was so worried about six months from now, I was letting the final hours slip through our fingers. I shed my apron. "Isabel! I need you and Marcus to watch the shop this morning. I will be back before lunch."

# CHAPTER NINE

*J* rushed up the front steps and into the lobby of the Lodge, realizing, as my eyes searched the lobby, I didn't have the first clue as to how to find Layton. Both Alma and my father had said he'd been beside himself the night before, but I knew his character. He would be in his sessions or performing whatever other obligation he'd made to the summit.

He wouldn't let the queen or the children down. It wasn't in his nature.

In the far corner of the lobby I saw Delilah lining up the children making sure scarves were tied, hats were covering ears, and gloves were on.

I hurried to her. "Are all of you leaving?"

She scowled. I couldn't blame her. Causing Layton pain had irritated many people it would seem. Her arms tightly crossed in front of her chest. "I'm taking the children out for a skiing lesson, provided by the conference. Our flight isn't until tomorrow morning."

"I need to talk to Layton."

Her glare burrowed through me. I could see the question

in her eyes. I started to explain I was here to make things right, but was interrupted by a tug on my jacket.

I looked down into Hannah's hopeful eyes.

"Prince Layton missed you at dinner last night."

I squatted down to eye level. "I missed eating with all of you, honey. I had a lot on my mind and needed time alone to think."

"Is that what you need to talk to Prince Layton about?" Delilah asked.

"It is. Please, tell me where I can find him."

"He's with Mrs. Alscher and Mr. Bosco in his office."

"Thank you so much." I waved to the children before maneuvering the growing crowd—it appeared the skiing lessons were being offered to all the children, not just Layton's. It was a wonderful thing to do, but I didn't have time to focus on the royal family's kindness now.

I marched through the door Layton had taken me through the night before and maneuvered the hall, my single focus being Layton.

I was about halfway to my destination, when two men—who I'd come to know as the queen's security—came from one of the other rooms, followed by the queen and Garan trailing just a couple of steps behind.

When she saw me approach, she paused and called my name. "I'm so happy to see you. I just told Garan I needed to get in touch with you."

"You did?" I felt my eyes wander toward Layton's door. It was still early, but I knew he would have a full day within the summit. If I didn't talk to him soon, I might not get a chance until tonight.

I'd already left him on the hook too long.

"Do you have a minute to discuss some business in my office?"

*Can you say no to a queen?* I knew I couldn't, even if it was something that could legitimately be done.

She seemed to sense my hesitation, or maybe it was the way my eyes kept darting toward Layton's door.

He hand brushed my shoulder. "This will only take a moment. I promise."

"Of course," I followed her back into the room, arranged much like Layton's.

"The pastries you've made this week brought back some very fond memories for my husband. At first bite, he said they reminded him of the ones his family enjoyed years ago. When I mentioned that to Alma, she made us aware you were the daughter of James and Viviana. Maybe I should have made that connection given the name of your bistro. My entire family has such fond memories of your mother."

Tears sprung to my eyes. My mother had been a constant thought this week. Hearing others tell me how the remembered her or her cooking always touched me in a deep way.

"Thank you for saying that. If I come even close to preparing my mother's recipes as well as she did, it is a good day."

"*An exact replica* is what Sinclair said. He insisted on taking some home to share with the rest of the family—who all said the same thing. They want to be able to have these treats again in the castle. Regularly."

*Was she asking me to come work for the crown? As my mother had?* As tempting as a regular paycheck—that came without worrying if I would be able to make ends meet—was, I knew immediately I couldn't let go of my dream. "I would love to be able to provide food for your royal highness's family—"

"Lovely!" She took my hands. "Thank you so much."

"But, I—"

"Don't worry. It is not our intention to overwhelm you.

We will give you as much notice as we can with our orders, but we expect them to be quite consistent."

*Orders. I was going to have steady orders to fill for the castle.* Knowing that lifted the heavy weight I'd been carrying. I would make my business work. Marcus and Isabella would have jobs. I may even have to hire more staff.

"Thank you, Queen Margaret."

"Oh! You're quite welcome. I know we threw a lot at you this week, and you've worked long, hard hours to help make this—my first summit—a success. I can't tell you what that means to me."

"I was honored."

She gave my wrist a little squeeze. "You will be hearing from Garan soon. Now, I will let you get to Layton." She punctuated the sentence with a wink and then left the room.

I didn't even take time to fully process everything this meant for *Viviana*'s. I spun on my heels and continued down the hall. I needed to talk to Layton. I needed to let him know I had the strength to fight hard to make things work between us.

I didn't even pause to knock on the door, just put my hand on the knob and pushed forward.

Alma, my father, and especially Layton, turned their attention to me. A light brightened Layton's eyes, and his smile left those adorable dimples in his cheeks. "I'm sorry to interrupt, but I need to talk to you."

"Of course." He turned to the others.

Before he could say a word, Alma stood. "We will give you some privacy. When you've finished, you can find us in the lobby."

I stepped to the side of the door to make room for the entourage.

My father paused and gave my wrist a squeeze as he

leaned in to whisper in my ear. "I'm glad to see you decided to come talk to him, whatever your decision is."

"No more fear," I whispered back and kissed his cheek.

He smiled at me, before letting go of my hand and leaving the room. When the door closed, I saw Layton's posture softened, but his face remained stoic, guarding his heart I supposed.

He rounded his desk, leaning back against it. "What is it you want to say?"

"First, I need to apologize. You worked very hard to come up with a way we could spend more time together. I didn't act very grateful."

"I shocked you. It was a lot to take in." So like Layton to give my feelings consideration, even though they had hurt him.

I took a step closer, resisting the urge to run and embrace him. There were things I had to say first. "All last night I wrestled with the reasons why this wouldn't work. I kept telling myself it was too much to ask you to do. I feared you would sacrifice everything about your life...and in the end, we might not work."

"For me, the risk is worth it."

"I'd never want you to resent me for the things you missed."

"I'd never."

His words touched me, warmed my insides, but I needed to spit out the speech I'd rehearsed on the drive up. "You are very important to me too. It scares me how fast my feelings developed. This morning, when I was talking to Mrs. Alscher, I realized it was more about the exchange of jobs or your position with your family. It was the *time*. Do you know how much can change in six months?"

"I'm counting on a lot changing in the time we're together." There was a passion in his eyes now, much like what I saw right before he kissed me the other night.

"My mother lost her life in a snap of my fingers. The same thing could happen to my father."

He stepped closer and reached out for me, but I held up my hand.

"Not yet. Let me finish talking."

He stopped in his tracks. "Sweet Georgianne, nothing in this life is promised."

"I know, and I don't want to live in fear. Whatever tomorrow brings I want to give you and me a real chance."

This time there was no stopping him, he closed the distance between us, and swept me up in his arms. "I'm so happy. Just so you know, this is going to be a wonderful experience on all levels." He slid back, and met my gaze. "Your father is very excited too."

"I know. We talked last night."

"You will be able to communicate with him."

"I know that, too, but I want to go see him. I want you to be able to see your family and your children."

"My family will adore you."

"Even if I'm just a common girl."

He kissed my forehead. "There is nothing ordinary about you. They will see that just as I have. We'll make it work. You'll see." He closed his arms around me again and I laid my head on his shoulder.

Maybe we were fighting a losing battle. Two people from two different worlds, but the best we could do was try.

I pledged to do just that. Wholeheartedly, I committed to my prince.

# EPILOGUE

*ive and a half months later.*

So much had changed since the end of the summit, but I had come quite familiar with my current surroundings. I sat in the small office I made for myself off the kitchen of my bistro. Across my desk sat the queen. We were discussing an order for the following weekend.

As of late, we met weekly. Sometimes, I would go to the castle, but just as often she came to me.

The royal family would be entertaining extended family and they wanted morning and afternoon deliveries made to the kitchen. Not just the desserts my little bistro was becoming well known for, but food from my newly expanded menu.

*Viviana's* was doing quite well. I'd doubled my staff a month after the summit and then recently had expanded it again. If things continued as they had, I would be extending my hours and adding a dinner menu.

The queen closed the folder in front of her and pushed it aside. "Thank you, Georgianne." She then handed another across the desk to me. "Before I go, I want to discuss the next summit, it will be here before we know it. I wanted to give you a chance to look over what I'd like to do with food."

I opened the folder and glanced at the projected requirements she was asking of me. "Will the lodge be okay with you getting so much food from me?"

"The lodge is one of my family's many business investments, the ultimate decision of the food served is up to us."

I didn't know what say, so I simply nodded. The praise I received still surprised me.

"With the success of the first summit under our belt, we look to have a thirty percent increase in attendees this year."

"That's wonderful."

There was a light knock on the open door, and I looked up to see my prince. He was leaned against the door looking very relaxed and very handsome, dressed in all black. "I hope I'm not interrupting."

The queen smiled and stood, gathering her things. "Not at all, Layton, we'd just finished."

"Are you ready for lunch?" He zeroed his gaze on mine. We'd developed the habit of having a quiet lunch in the dining room after I locked the doors for the day, and it was something we'd both grown to enjoy. Today, I felt as though he had something more up his sleeve. Layton looked as if he were about to burst with excitement.

"I will be in just a moment." I walked to the queen to the door, where her entourage waited. She turned back and waved goodbye before she got into the car.

When I twisted around to find Layton, I noticed our usual table was already set up with full pates, and candle light. "When did this happen?"

"I called Isabel and had her set it up while Margaret distracted you."

I slid into his arms, and he pulled me in leaving a warm kiss on my lips. "You spoil me."

"I try."

He led me to the table and we sat, but before taking a bite to eat, he reached across the table. I gave him my hands.

"Your father will be coming home in two weeks."

A pain shot through me. Sure, Layton and I had ups and downs in our developing relationship, but we'd also grown very deeply—very madly—in love, spending as much time as possible together.

As he'd predicted, he'd both learned from my father's program and made improvements as well.

From what my dad had told in me in many of our phone conversations, his experience had been similar. Despite the success, I knew Dad was excited to be coming home and returning to his previous job.

I knew Layton and I were committed to making our relationship work, but I still didn't know what that was going to look like when the exchange was over. Just the idea of spending long lengths of time away from him made my heart hurt.

"I suppose it's time to start thinking about the fact you will be returning to your country too."

Even I could hear the tears in my voice. By the expression on Layton's face, he heard them too.

"I do have to go home for a few weeks. I'm hoping you will be able to join me for at least part of it."

"A few weeks? And then what?"

"You know I can't just shirk my responsibilities to my country. I've served in the position I've held for a long time."

"And you are so good at it. Working with children is so much more than your job."

"I will be very excited to see my children and visit with them. I will also be helping Alma get orientated so she can take over for me."

*Wait. What?* "But why?"

"Margaret has offered me a position in her charity. I'm going to be staying in Montgomery."

"But...but..." All the old questions of what Layton was sacrificing rose to the surface, stealing my ability to speak.

"It is a good position in which I can do a lot to help many children. The bonus is I get to stay close to my fiancé. That is, if you will have me."

He slid an open black velvet box across the table. In it was a beautiful white gold ring encrusted with diamonds, rubies and emeralds. "Will you do me the honor of becoming my bride?"

I raised a hand, covering my mouth.

My love for my prince bubbled up in my chest, pressing down those knee-jerk fears and concerns. I was strong, and so was Layton. We'd found a way to make the previous five and a half months work, and I was confident we could make the next sixty or more years work just as well.

"I'd love nothing more."

Layton's smile widened, and he took the ring from the box and slipped it on my finger. "My entire family is looking forward to seeing you again. Do you think you might be able to join me in Ronaria for the second half of my trip?"

"I will find a way."

When Layton had first come to Montgomery, he'd been hoping he would be able to blend into the fabric of the queen's summit. He'd wanted a royal holiday—a chance to live outside of the spotlight. In his time here, we'd both discovered—limelight or not—whatever life brought us, the joy would be in experiencing it together.

# RAISING THE ROYAL BARRE
## CHAPTER 1

I took the tray from Georgianne and held it as she moved her now-famous lemon tarts to the display case. My boisterous and chatty boss had been uncharacteristically quiet this morning, and I couldn't help but worry.

I knew she was no different than the rest of us—even if she was now engaged to Ronaria's Prince Layton—but her sullen mood sent a wave of nausea through my stomach.

Something wasn't right.

When Georgianne opened *Viviana's Bistro* a couple of years ago, sales had been unstable. She'd obsessed over the business she'd named in honor of her late mother, over the daily receipts and expenditures, to the point I feared for my job.

I knew she was as loyal to me as I was to her. We were, after all, sisters, in a not-by-blood sort of way. You see, her father served as a top administrator at the orphanage I'd grown up in. I might have been a child of the system, never finding a home of my own after being removed from my mother's care at the age of nine, but James Bosco and his wife, Viviana, had provided temporary respite on the occasions I found myself between arrangements stamped *permanent foster situations.*

The longest lasted six months.

The feelings of being lost and abandoned had cultivated a need in me. One I finally felt mature and stable enough to pursue. I wanted to provide a safe and loving home to an older child—one like me—who was less likely to find a family to call their own otherwise.

Not like my own mother who chose drugs, alcohol, and revolving men over me. Not like the too-numerous-to-count foster families whose love I learned was conditional on my behavior.

Not for brief spans of time. Forever.

The way a parent was supposed to love a child.

James and Viviana were the closest thing to parents I'd ever known, and Georgianne had been a loving and supportive big sister—protecting me when necessary—most often from myself.

Before I'd been removed from my mother's home, I'd been the type of child who worked so hard to please others, believing if I could make Mom happy she would love me enough. After the official children's services came, my attitude spun one-hundred-eighty degrees. I rebelled, pushed boundaries, and acted out to build walls and prove the misguided notion I was unlovable.

The only ones who didn't react as I expected—and send me back into the system—were the Boscos. Instead they would take me in until James's team could find another placement for me. He never gave up on me or the idea I could be reached and helped.

When I aged out of the system and needed a job, Georgianne didn't hesitate to hire me. It didn't matter her budget didn't allow for an employee, she found a way to keep me on.

No one was happier than me was when she found her literal Prince Charming.

Ronaria's Prince Layton—in town for Queen Margaret's child welfare summit—had walked into the bistro and swept Georgianne off her feet.

The two were from different worlds, but they had proved love could win out when each partner was willing to work at it. Both made allowance and sacrifices so they could be together.

Because Layton was the sixth-in-line—and not likely to take the throne—he'd been able to move to Montgomery so Georgianne could keep the coffee shop and be near her father.

Ever since, business had grown steadily. I'd even heard the couple discussing a second location in recent weeks, which was why Georgianne's mood puzzled me.

One thing I knew for sure, good things never last. If Georgianne was worried, there was cause to be. Not knowing how to broach the subject, I reached for a colloquial doorway. "Penny for your thoughts."

Georgianne's attention snapped to me, and she forced a smile. "It's obvious that I'm preoccupied. Isn't it?"

"A little."

"Quinton is arriving today for a visit."

My mouth went dry and I swallowed hard. Before I'd ever heard of Layton Kotnic, Prince of Ronaria, I'd known of—idolized—Prince Quinton Kotnic, ballet dancer. Though I was never *really* good at it, Viviana enrolled me in dance classes when I lived with them, and I'd fallen in love, searching the internet for videos of performances.

In one performance from the National Slovakian Ballet company Quinton had danced as guest principal.

He'd seemed to drop off the world stage a few years ago, and I'd wondered what happened, I'd often thought of asking

Layton about his brother, but never wanted to breech his sense of privacy when it came to his family. "Layton's brother?"

"The next oldest, the one he's closest to."

"Layton must be excited to see him."

"He is. We're both worried he's delivering a plea for us to return to Ronaria."

Layton had devoted his life to children's welfare before deciding to relocate to Montgomery. Nothing had changed since—he first worked in our country's child welfare departments and later took a position in our queen's charitable foundation. Both positions enhanced his likability on the world stage. It seemed everyone admired him for his humanitarian efforts and extreme modesty. Layton didn't thrive in the spotlight like Quinton once had; in fact, he avoided it as much as possible.

I suppose that's why he seemed blissfully happy in his new life. Until this moment, I believed Layton had the full support of his royal siblings and parents. "Why would the family want him home, if that's not where he wants to be?"

"We don't know for sure that is the reason for his visit. The guise seems to be to bring us a housewarming gift, but I can't help but worry. I can tell Layton is nervous too."

If Quinton persuaded Layton to return to Ronaria, there was no question Georgianne would follow. A year ago, my boss might have chosen her business over romance, but these twelve months of Layton's love had molded her. She would follow him around the globe.

Georgianne took the empty tray from my hands. "I'm going to put this away and make a few calls. Sitting here waiting for Quinton to arrive will only drive me crazy."

I felt my knees nearly buckle. "He's coming here?"

"Queen Margaret is sending a car as a favor to Layton. We'll all meet up here."

"If it helps, I can finish the prep work and open the doors."

Georgianne touched my shoulder. "I have full faith in you, Isabel. The other girls will be here shortly. Turn on the lights, set the register, and open the doors as soon as all of you are ready."

I picked up the frilly white apron from under the counter and tied it in place. I'd been skeptical of the new uniforms Layton suggested six months ago. I was sure the black pencil skirt and black dress shirt would show every speck of flour and sugar and the white frills of the apron would be easily caught and torn, but they'd proven to be durable. I'd even grown fond of the higher-end look they gave the shop.

Today, I was grateful for the neat, clean appearance, and ran my fingers over my hair hoping it was all tucked neatly into my ponytail. I'd never imagined I ever see Quinton Kotnic in person, let alone have the chance to speak with him.

Jana and Lenore filed in from the back just as I finished setting the register for the day, so I crossed the room and flipped the switch that lit up the sign and windows.

As I twisted the lock, I noticed the man who I'd watched dance on my computer screen countless times climb out of a black sedan bearing the emblem of the Royal Family of Montgomery on the door. For the first time, I noticed the striking similarity between him and his brother, yet the differences were just as obvious. Quinton was a longer, leaner version of his sibling. Where Layton's posture and stance could only be described as royal, Quinton carried himself in a way exuding strength and poise.

As the man approached, I held the door. I'd like to say I remembered everything I'd been taught about properly respecting a member of a royal family when I curtseyed, but it was more because my nerves got the best of me. "You must be Prince Quinton of Ronaria."

He touched my arm and held my gaze. My flesh warmed beneath his hand. "Please. There is no need for formalities."

I let go of the door, letting it glide shut. His green eyes held an intensity I'd never seen. Though he smiled warmly, he looked weighted down by something. I couldn't help but wonder if Georgianne was spot-on with her concerns.

Even though his presence might inevitably cost me my job a tingle still crawled my spine and my stomach fluttered when our eyes met.

Not knowing what to say, I simply nodded.

He looked to the nametag on my shoulder. "Isabel. Lovely name for a beautiful woman."

*A smooth talker, this one.* I called out to Jana. "Would you tell Georgianne Prince Quinton is here?"

"What did I tell you about formalities?"

Though he seemed to protest the title—much like Layton did—Quinton's modesty rang false. He walked past me, and I rounded the counter, trying my best to make a good impression on Georgianne's behalf. "Would you like something? A cup of coffee?"

"A double shot of espresso would be wonderful. It was a dreadfully long trip."

I picked up a cup and placed it on the tray on the large stainless-steel machine. Working my way through the steps, I steeled myself. Just being in the same room with the object of my dance obsession made my head spin, and I fought the desire to turn back and soak in the man's muscular frame and good looks.

*Don't forget he's here to convince Layton to go home, which in turn would close this shop and cost me my job.*

Once I had the brewing process started, I turned back to the counter and picked up a plate and the tongs. I opened the case and placed an assortment of our most popular treats on the plate: a lemon tart, an apple blossom, a cannoli, and a chocolate cookie." I carried the plate around the counter and motioned for Quinton to follow me. "You and Georgianne can sit over here. She will be right out, and I'll bring you your espresso as soon as it's ready."

He paused in front of the table, his stare causing my body to flush. "Thank you for your hospitality, but I don't have the same sweet tooth my brother does."

"Really?" I motioned to the cookie. "Who doesn't like chocolate?"

Georgianne approached. "Quinton doesn't. Can you bring me a cup of coffee and a blueberry scone for him?"

"That would be nice," he responded and then opened his arms to Georgianne. "It is so good to see you."

I noticed she wavered before stepping into his embrace. Her hesitance clicked off a warning alarm. Was Georgianne really worried about Quinton's visit, or had she not been as warmly accepted by the royal family of Ronaria as I once believed?

Still a lick of jealousy settled low in my stomach as Quinton closed the embrace. I quickly shook it off, turning back to the counter to fulfill Georgianne's request.

At the counter, I placed the scone on a plate and filled a cup with coffee as I watched Quinton step back while keeping his hands on Georgianne's shoulders.

His entire focus seemed to be on his soon-to-be sister-in-law; I couldn't take my eyes off him.

I picked up the plate and mug, set to go back to the table, when Jana interrupted my train of thought. "Can you tell Georgianne Layton is on the phone?"

"Certainly." As I approached the table again, Quinton said, "Mother ordered me to inquire on the date for the nuptials."

Georgianne twisted her hands. "Your brother and I have narrowed it down to early fall."

"Of this year?" Quinton laughed. "Do you know how long it takes to plan a royal affair?"

Georgianne shrugged. "Have you met your brother? He's insisting on as low-key wedding as possible."

I set the plate on the table in front of Quinton and the mug in front of Georgianne. "Layton is on the phone for you."

She slipped from the booth. "Can you sit and keep Quinton company?"

He didn't look like the type who needed to be monitored. I wondered if Georgianne was adhering to some sort of royal protocol I wasn't aware of. She'd grown quite comfortable with all the etiquette between her interactions with Montgomery's and Ronaria's royal families, I would take her lead and trust her guidance, even though I was sure my nerves would cause me to misspeak and say something stupid. I slid into the booth and found myself lost in the prince's bright green eyes.

He watched Georgianne disappear through the door to the kitchen. "She keeps herself very busy."

"It's her bistro. She's always been very hands on."

He smirked and broke off a piece of the scone with a fork. "And that's why Georgianne is a perfect match for Layton. She shies away from the limelight almost as much as he does."

Modesty *was* a suit Layton wore well, and it was a trait I adored about him. I always imagined his humility came from the way he was raised. Meeting Quinton now, I wondered if my assessment was true.

"Just like with this wedding," he continued. "Where does he get the idea they can have something simple and private?"

"From what Georgianne tells me, neither wants money

spent on a ceremony that could be used to help the people of Ronaria."

"Neither my parents nor their subjects will allow their wedding to be anything but a stunning event." Quinton broke off another piece of the scone. After chewing thoroughly and swallowing, he said. "It might take some time, but Georgianne will come to learn what it means to be royal and what her and my brother's marriage means to our country."

My stomach twisted into tighter knots. The way he spoke, Georgianne's worse fears seemed to be coming true. I wanted to be sympathetic to what this would mean for the woman I'd come to think of as my sister, but I was preoccupied by how this would affect me and my plans to adopt.

If Layton returned to Ronaria once they were married, Georgianne would have to either sell or close the restaurant. Without a job, not only would I have to put my immediate plans on hold, but my ability to pay my rent would be called into question.

If I were to continue entertaining Quinton, maybe it would be best for my sanity if I changed the subject. "Georgianne mentioned you head up Ronaria's art council."

He nodded. "I do. It's not really all that interesting to be honest. I'm sure you would enjoy talking to my two oldest brothers more. They are more like Layton."

It seemed he was trying to downplay his role in his family's rule of their small nation. At first, Quinton seemed standoffish, now I wondered if was just uncomfortable in the unfamiliar surroundings. It hadn't been *that* long since he'd stepped away from dancing. "I try to follow politics and be informed about the world around me, but honestly, I'm much more interested in dancing and the arts. I find it sad some countries are cutting the arts out of their public schools."

He stiffened. "Did Georgianne tell you about my former life?"

I pulled my lower lip between my teeth, wondering if I should admit my admiration. Honesty quickly won out. "She didn't have to. I'm a longtime fan of your work."

His shoulders relaxed, and he eased back into his seat, reaching into his suit jacket. For the first time since he came into the restaurant, his smile seemed genuine, pushing up his cheeks and lighting up his eyes. "It's wonderful to meet someone who has an appreciation."

Pulling out his phone, he woke it up and clicked at the screen a few times, before turning it toward me. "I was in Slovakia a few weeks ago visiting with my friends from their national ballet. There, I found these pieces done by a local artist. There are four pictures. Slide left."

I thumbed through the pictures of snowy landscapes done with such bright colors and crisp lines I could feel the arctic chill the artist tried to convey. "These are beautiful."

"I hope Layton likes them. They are a housewarming gift for Georgianne and him."

"I'm sure he will love them."

"My hope is they remind him of home."

Fear pinged through me again. The only reason to remind Layton of home would be to encourage him to return. I pushed back against my desire to outright ask if he was on a mission to stir up my life. "I'm ashamed to admit I knew very little about Ronaria until we met Layton. I do know Slovakia is a close neighbor. The landscape must be similar?"

"Don't be ashamed, we are but a blip on the map. The rest of the world finds it easy to ignore us." His hand brushed against mine sending an electrical charge through me.

I tried to ignore my need to be touched by him again and returned his phone. "From the way Layton speaks, it sounds like a lovely country. He talks about the philanthropic work you and all your brothers do. You should be proud."

He visibly cringed. "Layton works hard to make the world a better place. My role seems to be fundraising for the sake of art and culture."

"It can be a cruel world, we need all the beauty we can get."

His gaze bore through me. He seemed to be contemplating my words, considering me. I felt exposed under his stare. Could he read my thoughts? Could he tell how attracted I was to him? Something out of the corner of his eye caught his attention, and he slid out of the booth, standing.

I started to rise, but Georgianne came into my line of sight, waving for us to stay seated. "Layton is dealing with a crisis. He hopes to be here soon."

"They couldn't even give me the chance to talk to Layton myself. Who called? Was it Brodrick or Adrian?"

Georgianne tipped her head. "Why would your brothers be calling about the earthquake in Italy that leveled an orphanage?"

Quinton looked as though he wanted to kick himself. He fidgeted with his jacket, trying to flatten wrinkles that weren't there. "Because they know Layton would be concerned."

Quinton's response slid by me, all I could focus on was the tragedy Georgianne had mentioned. "Oh no! Leveled? Were there any casualties?"

Georgianne's eyes drifted closed. Her horror was evident on her face. "It's only happened within the hour. There are three missing, and six children injured. The rest are accounted for and shaken up but fine." Georgianne turned her attention to Quinton, laying her hand on his shoulder. "Details of the earthquake haven't hit the news yet. You thought your brothers called about something else. Layton and I are excited that you're here, but I *am* confused. Is there more to this? Is there something going on in Ronaria we should know about?"

He gave a curt nod. "I would prefer to discuss it with both of you at once. How much longer will he be?"

"A half hour is what he hoped. They were just getting some first reports, and he and our queen wanted to set a team to start organizing the initial responses. As soon as they have a plan of action, he will be able to take a break."

With the turn in the conversation, I felt like an outsider looking in on a family meeting. I stood. "I should get back to work."

Georgianne turned to me. "Thank you for keeping Quinton company for me. I know I can always count on you."

"Yes," he said. "I would like to continue our discussion later."

Was he being polite, or did he really want to see me again? The mere thought had my cheeks flushing. "That would be nice."

I turned to Georgianne. "It sounds like Margaret, Layton, and the others at the foundation are going to be very busy today. Should I send food?"

Georgianne gave me a warm smile. "I already thought about that. Layton said he didn't think it would be necessary. There is only so much they can do at the moment. I want to talk to Layton first, but I think we may see what we can do to send food to the victims."

"Just let me know what needs to be done."

"I will."

Quinton pulled his phone out of his breast pocket again. "If you'll excuse me, I'm going to call Father and see if he has any more insight on the matter."

I watched the prince cross the restaurant with strong, confident strides. He sat at a stool at the counter and dialed the phone.

When he spoke, he did so in his native language. Even though I didn't understand a word he said, I could hear the emotion. It appeared to me he was talking to someone about something more personal and painful than a country miles away from his own.

Either Quinton was more affected by the tragedy than he immediately let on, or Georgianne's hunch was right and there was more to his visit than he'd originally indicated.

Buy Raising the Royal Barre

# ACKNOWLEDGMENTS

*Thank you*:

Dear reader for picking up this book. I hope you enjoyed this little escape.

I would love to hear what you think and hope you will review the story.

As always, thank you to my family. Brad Phillips, Josh Phillips, Katelynn Phillips, and Jessica Phillips. Without your support I wouldn't be able to continue putting out these books.

To my crew! Those of you who read, review, comment, and share! You guys are awesome.

Gilly Wright for your amazing red pen skills!

# ABOUT CONSTANCE PHILLIPS

Constance Phillips lives in Ohio with her husband, daughter, and four canine kids where she writes contemporary romance novels and paranormal romance novels.

When not writing stories of finding and rediscovering love, Constance and her husband spend the hours planning a cross-country motorcycle trip for the not-so-distant future...if they can find a sidecar big enough for the pups.

# CONNECT WITH CONSTANCE

*You can find news and information about new releases, appearances, signings, etc at the following places. (Links at Constancephillips.com)*

- Newsletter
- Website
- Facebook
- Instagram

# MORE BOOKS BY CONSTANCE PHILLIPS

**RONARIA'S ROYALS**
Royal Holiday
Raising the Royal Barre

**THE REALM'S SALVATION SERIES**
Fairyproof
Council Courtship (Novella)
Chasing Power

**SUNNYDALE DAYS SERIES**
All That's Unspoken
All That's Unclaimed
All That's Unrealized
All That's Unforgiven
All That's Unforeseen

**SUNNYDALE WEDDINGS (NOVELLAS)**
Nate and Hailey

**ANTHOLOGY**

Lexi's Chance (free with subscription to newsletter)

## TO PROTECT AND SERVE
Love Reclaimed
Lone Star Leave (Novella)

## SINGLE TITLE BOOKS
Resurrecting Harry
The Ultimate Catch
Refused to Reign